LOVE
STORIES

KINGFISHER
Larousse Kingfisher Chambers Inc.
95 Madison Avenue
New York, New York 10016

First edition 1997
2 4 6 8 10 9 7 5 3 1

LIBRARY OF CONGRESS CATALOGING-IN-PUBLICATION DATA
Love stories / chosen by Ann Pilling: illustrated by Aafke Brouwer.—
—1st American ed.
p. cm.—(Story library)
Summary: A collection of love stories encompassing romance, family
love, and legends, by such authors as Diana Wynne Jones, Oscar
Wilde, and Guy de Maupassant.
ISBN 0-7534-5117-4
1. Love stories. 2. Children's stories. [1. Love—Fiction.
2. Short stories.] I. Pilling, Ann. II. Brouwer, Aafke, ill.
III. Series.
PZ5.L84 1997
[Fic]—dc21 96-52714 CIP AC

Printed in Great Britain

LOVE
STORIES

CHOSEN BY
ANN PILLING

ILLUSTRATED BY
AAFKE BROUWER

Kingfisher
NEW YORK

CONTENTS

THE MISSING VITAL ORGAN   7
Betsy Byars (from *Bingo Brown and the Language of Love*)

THE GREEN BEHIND THE GLASS   13
Adèle Geras

CINDERELLA GIRL   30
Vivien Alcock

THE NIGHTINGALE AND THE ROSE   40
Oscar Wilde

LOVE LETTERS   48
Kate Walker

THE GIRL WHO LOVED THE SUN   54
Diana Wynne Jones

THE WORST KIDS IN THE WORLD (an extract)   75
Barbara Robinson

THE FAT GIRL'S VALENTINE   83
Ann Pilling (from *The Big Pink*)

A RAILWAY STORY   95
Guy de Maupassant

ORPHEUS AND EURYDICE   104
James Reeves (*A Greek myth*)

BILLIE   112
Ann Pilling

LUCKY LIPS   128
Paul Jennings

A STAR FOR THE LATECOMER (an extract)   140
Paul Zindel and Bonnie Zindel

THE PLATE: A QUESTION OF VALUES   154
Geraldine McCaughrean (from *A Pack of Lies*)

A PROPOSALE   167
Daisy Ashford (from *The Young Visiters*)

I WAS ADORED ONCE, TOO   171
Jan Mark

FOR BEING GOOD   190
Cynthia Rylant

THE WATER WOMAN AND HER LOVER   196
Ralph Prince (*A Guyanese legend*)

THE FAVORITE   204
Jacqueline Wilson

TELLING STORIES   213
Maeve Binchy

Acknowledgments   223

THE MISSING
VITAL ORGAN

BETSY BYARS

from Bingo Brown and the Language of Love

BINGO HAD A STRANGE, empty feeling.

It wasn't hunger. He ate and he still had it. It wasn't thirst. He drank a lot of pop, too. Bingo didn't know exactly what it was. It was just a huge internal void.

It was as if some vital organ had been secretly removed from his body and beamed up to some alien. And now this alien was stretched out contentedly, saying, "Ah," while on earth Bingo suffered in confusion.

Perhaps, Bingo thought, he could use this empty feeling later in one of his science fiction novels, but now he could only wait for it to pass.

This was the third day of the emptiness. It had started that terrible afternoon when his mother had mistaken the incident in the kitchen for a romantic encounter. Ever since then, there had been this emptiness, which was not improving. If anything, he was getting more empty.

Bingo got up from the sofa. He said, "Come on, Misty.

7

Let's go to the store."

At the sight of her leash, Misty began trembling with excitement.

"Don't get your hopes up. I'm just going for some noodles and a can of tuna. Tonight I'm making tuna lasagna."

Bingo hooked the leash on Misty's rhinestone collar. He was glad to have Misty these days. With this terrible three-day emptiness, he needed both companionship and eye contact. Misty's eyes watered a lot, so it was especially satisfying to tell her his troubles.

He and Misty were going down the steps when the mailman arrived. "I'll take those," Bingo said. He glanced down and stopped.

The top letter had his name on it. Mr. Bingo Brown. He loved the way his name looked with a *Mr.* in front of it. A name like Bingo needed a *Mr.*

He lifted the envelope and held it in his hand, as if weighing it. He smelled it for the scent of gingersnaps, but the letter only smelled like U.S. mail.

Bingo wondered if he would be able to control himself when Melissa started using perfume. If the scent of gingersnaps sometimes drove him mad, what would perfume—which was a chemical actually designed to drive men mad—do to him? Could he—

Misty whined at the end of her leash.

"In a minute, Misty."

He put the rest of the mail in the box and, slipping the end of the leash on his wrist like a bracelet, he opened his letter.

Dear Bingo,

I was really glad to get your letter, because after your phone calls stopped, I thought you had forgotten I was alive.

I've seen my new school, but I know I'm not going to like it as much as Roosevelt Middle School. For one thing, you won't be there.

A girl in my apartment building says the science teacher is neat. As you know, I'm going to be a scientist and a rock star, so this is important to me.

Bingo stopped for a moment, remembering the day Melissa had announced her dual careers to the class. "I am going to be a scientist and a rock star." It had been like a movie he had seen recently, and he had fallen instantly in love with Dr. Jekyll and Ms. Hyde.

He went back to the letter.

I wrote Mr. Mark a letter, giving him my new address, but he hasn't written back yet.

I think of you a lot, Bingo. I hope sometime I'll get back to see you, or maybe you could come out to Bixby for a visit. You ask your mom and I'll ask mine.

Love forever,
Melissa

P.S. I asked my best friend, Cici, to come over and take a picture of you. You probably don't know Cici, but she knows you because I pointed you out to her in the hall one day. If you don't want to have the picture taken, you don't have to.

Bingo stopped at the corner. While waiting for traffic, he put the letter in his pocket. Then he picked up Misty so they could cross the street. He had already learned that Misty was so afraid of cars she tried to run under them for safety. Above all, he did not want to have to say to Billy Wentworth, "Remember that dog I was keeping for you? Well, she got run over."

He put Misty down on the sidewalk, and they continued walking.

Bingo said, "Misty, I could never go to Bixby. For one thing, my mom wouldn't let me. And also, Misty, I don't particularly want to go.

"Oh, I wouldn't mind going somewhere. I like to travel. A plane ride, even a train or bus trip would probably do me a lot of good right now."

He paused before he went on. "What I wouldn't like would be getting there ... being there ..."

He stumbled and gasped. Misty came to the end of her leash and looked around, her wet eyes startled.

"Oh, Misty," he said.

He clasped his free hand over his heart.

Now Bingo realized what had happened to him. He realized what the terrible, empty void was.

He looked up at the sky as if the answer had come directly from there.

Of course he was empty!

He had every right to feel empty!

He would be an inhuman beast if he didn't feel empty!

"Misty," Bingo said with infinite sadness. "I am no longer in love."

Misty was looking back at him, holding eye contact. Her tail trembled.

"I don't know how it happened. How could a person be in love for eternity, no, for infinity, and then—" he shrugged helplessly, "then, *nothing!*"

Misty waited.

"This is the first time in six, no, seven months that I've

10

been without a real burning desire, and I don't use that word "burning" lightly. No wonder I've been feeling terrible. I'm the kind of person who has to have a burning desire."

He picked Misty up and tucked her under his arm for comfort.

"Perhaps I won't have any trouble falling in love again. After all, one time I fell in love with three girls in ten minutes, and my dad still falls in love at drugstores and supermarkets. I got the gene from him.

"But, Misty, would anybody other than Melissa fall in love with me? Having Melissa fall in love with me was pretty much a miracle, to be honest with you, and how many miracles happen to a person in one lifetime?"

The Bi-Lo doors parted, and Bingo entered the store. He walked purposefully through Produce, Dairy Products, and Cold Cuts.

"I must do one thing before I get the noodles. I want to go to the cookie aisle and smell the gingersnaps. This is a test, Misty. Because if I don't feel like calling Melissa when I smell gingersnaps, then I'll know for sure. See, the first time I rode in a car with Melissa—our substitute teacher was taking us to the hospital to visit Mr. Mark—as we got in the car, Melissa brushed against me, and I smelled gingersnaps. Ever since then . . ."

Bingo trailed off and reached for the gingersnap box. He took it down and stood looking at the picture of the round, cheerful, brown cookies.

An expression of sorrow came over Bingo's face. He returned the box gently to the shelf.

"Yes," he told Misty, "it's over."

As Bingo got his groceries and headed for the checkout counter, he thought how life had a way of U-turning.

At one time in his life he had wanted desperately to fall out of love with Melissa. He had been in love with Melissa and Harriet and Mamie Lou at the time, and he would have given anything, anything to fall out of love with any of them; he didn't even care which.

Without thinking about it twice, he would have put in his journal under:

TRIUMPHS OF TODAY

1. Falling out of love with Melissa.

But times had changed; life had made one of its cruel U-turns. Now he would put it firmly under TRIALS.

THE GREEN BEHIND
THE GLASS

ADÈLE GERAS

1916 November

THE TELEGRAM WAS ADDRESSED to Enid. Sarah put it carefully on the table in the hall. The white envelope turned red in the light that fell through the colored squares of glass above the front door. She had no desire to open it. She knew that Philip was dead. The possibility that he might be wounded, missing, captured, never occurred to her. It was death she had been expecting, after all. These were only the official words setting it out in writing. For a moment, Sarah wondered about the people whose work it was every day to compose such messages. Perhaps they grew used to it. The telegraph boy, though, couldn't meet her eyes.

"Telegram for Miss Enid Hurst," he'd said.

"I'll take it. I'm her sister. They're all out."

"Much obliged, I'm sure." He had thrust the envelope into her hand and run toward the gate without looking back, his boots clattering on the pavement. The envelope had fluttered suddenly in a rush of wind.

Sarah sat on the oak settle in the hall and wondered whether to take the message to Enid in the shop. To them, she thought, to the writers of this telegram, Philip is Enid's young man. He was. Was. Haven't we been embroidering and stitching and preparing for the wedding since before the War? Enid will enjoy mourning, thought Sarah. It will become her. She will look elegant in black, and she'll cry delicately so as not to mar the whiteness of her skin, and dab her nose with a lace-edged handkerchief, and wear Mother's jet brooch, and all the customers will sigh and say how sad it is, and young men will want to comfort and console her, and they will, oh yes, because she didn't really love him.

"She didn't really love him," Sarah shouted aloud in the empty house, and blushed as if there were a part of Enid lurking somewhere that could overhear her. "Not really," she whispered. "Not like I did." I know, she thought, because she told me.

> Enid is sewing. I ask her: "Do you really love him, Enid? Does your heart beat so loudly sometimes that you feel the whole world can hear it? Can you bear it, the thought of him going away? Do you see him in your dreams?"
>
> "Silly goose, you're just a child." She smiles at me. She is grown-up. Her face is calm. Pale. "And you've been reading too many novels. I respect him. I admire him. I am very fond of him. He is a steady young man. And besides, ladies in real life don't feel those things, you know. It wouldn't be right."

But I felt them, thought Sarah. And other feelings, too, which made me blush. I turned away, I remember, so that Enid should not see my face, and thought of his arms holding me, and his hands in my hair and his mouth . . . oh, such a melting, a melting in my stomach. I loved him. I can never say anything. I shall only be able to weep for him at

14

night, after Enid has fallen asleep. And I shall have to look at that photograph that isn't him at all, just a soldier in uniform, sepia, like all the soldiers. Enid will keep it there between our beds. Perhaps she will put it in a black frame, but after a while, I shall be the only one who really sees it.

Sarah tried to cry and no tears would come. It seemed to her that her heart had been crushed in metal hands, icy cold and shining. How could she bear the tight pain of those hands? But soon, yes, she would have to take the telegram and walk to the shop and watch Enid fainting and Mother rustling out from behind the counter. Mrs. Feathers would be there. She was always there, and she would tell, as she had told so often before, the remarkable story of her Jimmy, who'd been posted as dead last December and who, six months later, had simply walked into the house, bold as you please, and asked for a cup of tea.

"You're mine now," Sarah said aloud to the telegram, and giggled. Maybe I'm going mad, she thought. Isn't talking to yourself the first sign? I don't care. I don't care if I am mad. I shall go and change into my blue dress, just for a little while. Later, I shall have to wear dark colors, Philip, even though I promised you I wouldn't. Mother will make me wear them. What will the neighbors say, otherwise?

"Philip is like a son to me," Mother used to say, long before he proposed to Enid. "One of the family." Perhaps that is why he proposed. Or perhaps Mother arranged the whole thing. She is so good at arranging. Enid is piqued, sometimes, by the attention Philip pays to me. I am scarcely more than a child. Mother says: "But of course, he loves Sarah, too. Isn't she like a little sister to him?" When she says this, I clench my fists until the nails cut into my palms. I don't want that kind of love, no, not that kind at all.

15

Sarah laid the blue dress on the bed, and began to take off her pinafore. The sun shone steadily outside, but the leaves had gone. Swiftly, she pulled the hatbox from under the bed, and lifted out her straw hat with the red satin ribbons. It was a hat for long days of blue sky, green trees and roses. I can't wear it in November, she thought. It had been wrapped in tissue paper, like a treasure. Sarah had looked at it often, remembering the afternoon in Kew Gardens, so long ago, a whole three months. She had thought of it as the happiest day of her life, a day with only a small shadow upon it, an insignificant wisp of fear, nothing to disturb the joy. But now Philip was dead, and that short-lived moment of terror spread through her beautiful memories like ink stirred into clear water.

Enid's sewing basket was on the chest of drawers. Sarah was seized suddenly with rage at Philip for dying, for leaving her behind in the world. She took the dressmaking scissors out of the basket, and cut and cut into the brim of the hat until it hung in strips, like a fringe. The ribbons she laid beside her on the bed and she crushed the crown in her hands until the sharp pieces of broken straw pricked her,

hurt her. Then she snipped the long, long strips of satin into tiny squares. They glittered on her counterpane like drops of blood. When she had finished, her whole body throbbed, ached, was raw, as if she had been cutting up small pieces of herself. She lay back on the bed, breathless. I must go to the shop, she told herself. In a little while. If I close my eyes, I can see him. I can hear his voice. And Enid's voice. Her voice was so bossy, that day:

"You can't wear that hat," Enid says. "It's too grown-up."

"I am grown-up." I dance round the kitchen table, twirling the hat on my hand, so that the ribbons fly out behind it. "I shall be seventeen at Christmas, and it's just the hat for Kew."

"I don't know why you're coming, anyway," says Enid.

"She's coming because it's a lovely day, and because I invited her," Philip says.

He is leaning against the door, smiling at me.

"Thank you, kind sir." I sweep him a curtsy.

"A pleasure, fair lady," he answers, and bows gracefully.

"When will you two stop clowning?" Enid is vexed. "You spoil her all the time. I've had my hat on for fully five minutes."

"Then let us go," he says, and offers an arm to Enid and an arm to me.

In the street, Enid frowns: "It's not proper. Walking along arm-in-arm . . . like costermongers."

"Stuff and nonsense," says Philip. "It's very jolly. Why else do you suppose we have two arms?" I laugh. Enid wrinkles her nose.

"August is a silly time to come here." There is complaint in Enid's voice. She is sitting on a bench between me and Philip. "The camellias are long since over, and I love them so much. Even the roses are past their best." She shudders. "I do dislike them when all the petals turn brown and flap about in that untidy way."

"Let's go into the Glass House." I jump up and stand in front of them. Enid pretends to droop.

"Philip," she sighs, "you take her. I don't think I could bear to stand in that stifling place ever again, among the drips and smells."

Philip rises reluctantly, touches Enid's shoulder.

"What about you, though," he says. "What will you do?"

"I shall sit here until you return." Enid spreads her skirts a little. "I shall look at all the ladies and enjoy the sunshine."

"We'll be back soon," I say, trying to keep my voice from betraying my excitement. Have I ever before been alone with him? Will I ever be alone with him again? Please, please, please, I say to myself, let the time be slow, don't let it go too quickly.

Philip and I walk in silence. I am afraid to talk, afraid to open my mouth in case all the dammed-up love words that I am feeling flood out of it.

We stand outside the Glass House for a moment, looking in at the dense green leaves pressing against the panes. A cloud passes over the sun, darkens the sky, and we are both reflected in the green. Philip's face and mine, together. In the dark mirror we turn toward each other. I stare at his reflection, because I dare not look at him, and for an instant his face disappears, and the image is of a death's head grinning at me, a white skull: bones with no flesh, black sockets with no eyes. I can feel myself trembling. Quickly, I look at the real Philip. He is there. His skin is brown. He is alive.

"What is it, Sarah? Why are you shaking?"

I try to laugh, and a squeak comes from my lips. How to explain? "I saw something reflected in the glass," I say.

"There's only you and me."

"It was you and me, but you . . . you had turned into a skeleton."

The sun is shining again. Philip's face is sad, shadows are in his eyes as he turns to look. I look too, and the skull has vanished. I let out a breath of relief.

"It's only me, after all," he says.

"But it *was* there. I saw it so clearly. Philip, please don't die."

"I shan't," he says seriously, carefully. "I shan't die. Don't be frightened. It was only a trick of the light."

I believe him because I want to believe him. He takes my hand. "Let's go in," he says.

Inside the Glass House, heat surrounds us like wet felt. Thickly about our heads a velvety, glossy, spiky, tangled jungle sucks moisture from the air. Leaves, fronds, ferns, and creepers glisten, wet and hot, and the earth that covers their roots is black, warm. Drops of water trickle down the panes of glass. The smell of growing is everywhere, filling our nostrils with a kind of mist. We walk between the towering plants. There is no one else there at all. A long staircase, wrought iron painted white, spirals upward, hides itself in green as it winds into the glass roof. Philip is still holding my hand, and I say nothing. I want him to hold it forever. I want his hand to grow into mine. Why doesn't he speak to me? We always laugh and joke and talk so much that Enid hushes us perpetually, and now he has nothing to say. I think: perhaps he is angry. He wants to sit with Enid in the cool air. He is cross at having to come here when his time with Enid is so short. He is leaving tomorrow, and I have parted them with my selfishness and my love. Tears cloud my eyes. I stumble, nearly falling. My hat drops to the ground. Philip's hand catches me round the waist. I clutch at his arm, and he holds me, and does not let me go when I am upright. We stand, locked together. "Sarah . . ." It is a whisper. "Sarah, I must speak." The hand about my waist pulls me closer. I can feel the fingers spread out now, stroking me. Philip looks away. "I can't marry Enid," he says. "It wouldn't be right."

"Why?" There are other words, but they will not come.

"I can't tell her," he mutters. "I've tried. I can't." He looks at me. "I shall write to her. Soon. It's a cowardly thing to do, but I cannot bear to face her . . . not yet. Not now. Sarah?"

"Yes?" I force myself to look up.

"Sarah, do you know," his voice fades, disappears, " . . . my feelings? For you?"

"Me?" My heart is choking me, beating in my throat.

"I . . . I don't know how to say it." He looks over my head, cannot meet my eyes. He says, roughly: "I've thought it and thought it, and I don't know how to say it." He draws me closer, close to him. I can feel his buttons through my dress. I am going to faint. I am dissolving in the heat, turning into water. His arms are around me, enfolding me. His mouth is on my hair, moving in my hair. Blindly, like a plant in search of light, I turn my face up, and his lips are there, on my lips, and my senses and my nerve ends and my heart and my body, every part of me, all my love, everything is drawn into the sweetness of his mouth.

Later, we stand together, dazed, quivering. I can feel his kiss still, pouring through me.

"Philip, Philip," I bury my head in his jacket. "I love you. I've always loved you." Half hoping he will not hear me. He lifts my face in his fingers.

"And I love you, Sarah. Lovely Sarah, I love you. I don't know how I never said it before. How did I make such a mistake?"

I laugh. Everything is golden now. What has happened, what will happen, Enid, the rest of the world, nothing is important.

"I'm only a child," I say smiling, teasing.

"Oh no," he says, "no longer. Not a child." He kisses me again, softly. His fingers are in my hair, on my neck, touching and touching me. I have imagined it a thousand times and it was not like this. Wildly, I think of us growing here in this hothouse forever, like two plants curled and twined into one another, stems interlocked, leaves brushing . . . I move away from him.

"We must go back," I say.

"Yes." He takes my hat from the ground and puts it on my head.

"You must promise me," he says, "never to wear mourning."

"Mourning?" What has mourning to do with such happiness?

"If I die . . ."

"You won't die, Philip." I am myself again now. "You said you wouldn't. I love you too much. You'll come back, and we'll love one another forever, and live happily ever after, just like a prince and princess in a fairy tale."

He laughs. "Yes, yes we will. We will be happy."

Walking back together to Enid's bench, we make plans. He will write to me. He will send the letters to Emily, my friend. I shall tell her everything. He will write to Enid. Not at once but quite soon. We can see Enid now. She is waving at us. We wave back.

"Remember that I love you," Philip whispers when we are nearly oh, nearly there. I cannot answer. Enid is too close. I sit on the bench beside her, dizzy with loving him.

"You've been away for ages," she says. "I was quite worried."

His voice is light, full of laughter. "There's such a lot to look at. A splendid place. You really should have come."

I am amazed at him. I dare not open my mouth. Here in the fresh air, I cannot look at Enid. The dreadfulness of what I am doing to her, what I am going to do to her makes me feel ill. But how can I live with my love pushed down inside me forever? Will she forgive us? Will we have to elope? Emigrate? There will be time enough to worry when she finds out, when Philip tells her. Now, my happiness curls through me like a vine. We set off again along the gravel paths. I have to stop myself from skipping. I remember, briefly, the skeleton I saw reflected in the glass, and I laugh out loud at my childish fear. It was only a trick of the light, just as Philip had said. A trick of the light.

There are stone urns near the Temperate House, and curved stone flowers set about their bases. A lady is sitting on a bench in the sunshine under a black silk parasol. The light makes jagged pools of color in the inky taffeta of her skirts, and her hat is massed with ostrich feathers like funeral plumes. She turns to look at us as we go by, and I see that her face is old: small pink lips lost in a network of wrinkles, eyes still blue, still young under a pale, lined brow. She wears black gloves to cover her hands and I imagine them veined and still under the fabric. She smiles at me and I feel a sudden shock, a tremor of fear.

Enid says: "Forty years out of date at least. Do you

think she realizes how out of place she looks?"

"Poor old thing," says Philip. "Rather like a pressed flower, all alone in the world." He whistles the tune *Mademoiselle from Armentières*. "How would you like it?"

"I hope," says Enid, "that if I ever wear mourning, I shall not be so showy. Ostrich feathers, indeed! Mutton dressed as lamb."

I look back at the old woman, marveling at Enid and Philip for finding her interesting enough to talk about. I feel pity for her, and a faint amusement, but she does not hold my attention. She is as remote from me, as strange, as if she belonged to another time. I start to run across the grass, as fast as I can. They are chasing me, yes, even Enid, dignity forgotten, is running and running. We stop under a tree, all of us breathless. Philip puts his hands on my waist and twirls me round. I glance fearfully at Enid, but she is smiling at us like an indulgent mother.

We walk home in the dusk. I must leave him alone with Enid at the gate. He kisses me good-bye on the cheek, like a brother, and I go indoors quickly. I am burning in the places where he touched me.

Sarah sat up. Slowly, like a sleepwalker, she gathered up the torn, bruised straw and the scraps of ribbon from the bed and the floor, and put them in the hatbox. When there is time, she thought, I shall burn them in the kitchen fire. She struggled into the blue dress and looked at herself in the mirror. What she saw was the face of a stranger who resembled her: mouth pulled out of shape, skin white, hair without color. She fastened, carefully, the buttons on her cuffs. Her skin, all the soft surfaces of her body, felt raw, scraped, wounded. I am wounded all over, she thought, and went slowly downstairs. She put the telegram in her pocket, and left the house.

1917 May

"I think James will come to call this afternoon." Enid's fingers made pleats in the lilac skirt she was wearing.

Sarah said: "Do you like him?"

Enid considered the question. The sisters were walking in Kew Gardens. Enid wanted to see the camellias. "Yes," she said at last, "he is a fine man." Sarah thought of James's solid body and long teeth, his black hair and the small brush of his mustache. Over the months, scars had slowly covered the sore places in her mind but sometimes, especially at Kew, the pain took her breath away. She should not, she knew, walk there so often, but she did. She should have avoided the Glass House, but she went there at every opportunity, and stood beside the streaming panes with her eyes closed, willing herself to capture something. Her feelings on that day had been so overpowering, had filled her with such sharp pleasure that always she hoped that their ghosts must still be lingering among the leaves.

Now, she looked at Enid. "I think," she said, "that he will suit you very well."

"He hasn't proposed to me yet," Enid said placidly. "Although I don't think it will be too long. In any case, I shall have to wait at least until November . . ." Her voice trailed away, losing itself among the branches.

"Philip," Sarah said (and the word felt strange in her mouth, an unfamiliar taste, like forgotten fruit), "Philip would be pleased to think you were happy."

"Do you think so, really?" Enid looked relieved. "Of course, I was heartbroken, heartbroken at his death. You remember? I fainted, there and then on the floor of the shop. I shall never forget it."

"Neither shall I," said Sarah.

Enid comes out from behind the counter. She says: "What's the matter, Sarah? Are you ill? You look so white. Why are you wearing that thin dress?"

Mother is talking to Mrs. Feathers. It is absorbing talk. I do not think they have seen me.

I say nothing. I give the envelope to Enid. She tears it open: a ragged fumbling of her hands, not like her at all.

"It's Philip," she says. "Philip is dead."

I watch, mesmerized, as she falls in a liquid movement to the ground.

Mother loosens Enid's collar, her waistband, brings out smelling salts. She is weeping noisily. Mrs. Feather says: "I'll put the kettle on for a cup of tea. Plenty of sugar, that's the thing for shock."

I envy my mother every tear she is shedding. I want to cry, and I cannot. The iron grip tightens round my heart.

"His letters," said Enid, "in the months before his death were quite different, you know. Did I ever tell you?"

"No."

"More formal. Veiled. Forever talking about an important matter which he would discuss on his next leave. Not so . . . devoted."

Sarah tried to stop herself from feeling happy at this revelation.

"His last letter was particularly strange," Enid went on. "He was going to tell me something, he said. He couldn't bear to wait another day, but then the letter finished in a scrawl, messy and rushed, because, I suppose, they had to go and capture some hill or bit of wood. I shall never know what it was."

"It doesn't matter now," said Sarah.

"It is vexing, however," Enid said. "I should have liked to know." Part of Sarah longed to tell her, to tell her everything. But she said nothing. They walked on, in the direction of the Temperate House.

"Look," said Sarah. "She's there again. The old lady."

"She looks," said Enid, "as though she hasn't moved

since last August. I do believe that is the same dress."

"And the same hat," Sarah added. "Perhaps it's a favorite. It is certainly smart, even though it's black."

"Come this way, Sarah. I don't want to walk past her."

"I do. I want to."

"Then I shall wait for you over there. Truly, I don't understand you sometimes."

I don't understand myself, Sarah thought. Why am I doing this? She began to follow the same path that they had taken before. She could almost hear Philip whistling "... *Mademoiselles from Armentières ... hasn't been kissed for forty years ... hasn't been kissed ...*" The air seemed colder. Sarah turned her head away a little as she passed the bench. The lady said: "Such a lovely day, my dear. Don't you think it's a lovely day?"

Under the black feathers, the lady smiled at her, and Sarah could see in her eyes long memories of past happiness, past youth, past love.

"Yes," she said. "Lovely."

"I've seen you here before," the lady said.

"I come quite often. I like it here."

"You had a hat with red ribbons, I remember. I remember many things, and I recall that hat, because I had one once, too, and when I saw you . . ." The lady looked down.

"Yes?"

"You will think it absurd. But there, at my age, I'm permitted to be a little foolish. I thought I was seeing a ghost. A ghost of myself, when I was young."

Sarah smiled, a little nervously. "I must go back to my sister now," she said. "I think your hat is lovely."

The lady smiled, nodded, did not answer.

Sarah walked back to where Enid was waiting. She glanced toward the Temperate House, but the old lady had gone. There was no sign of her anywhere.

Later, on their way home, Sarah and Enid passed by the Glass House. "Are you going in today?" Enid asked.

"No," said Sarah. "I'm only looking in."

She stared at her reflection in the pane dark with the darkness of the green behind it, and touched the veiling that trimmed her hat. At first she did not recognize herself. The veiling looked . . . could it be . . . like feathers? Surely her mouth was not so shrunken, nor her cheeks so white? Her hands seemed stiff, she looked old, she looked wrinkled, she looked—no, no, she couldn't, wouldn't look, like the faded old lady on the bench. A pressed flower, Philip had said. She shook her head, moved it closer to the glass, and the image changed. She was herself again. There was her hat, her own face, still young. She shivered. A trick of the light, that was all it was. Only a trick of the light.

"I don't think," she said to Enid as they walked through the tall wrought iron gates, "I don't think I shall be coming to Kew ever again."

CINDERELLA GIRL

VIVIEN ALCOCK

BELLA JONES DIDN'T LIKE Meg Hunter one little bit. She was too rough, too noisy, and too grubby.

"It's not only the way she crashes about, knocking things over," she said. "It's everything about her. She always looks such a fright. That great bush of hair, I bet she never combs it. And her face is often *dirty*. As for her clothes! She came to school yesterday with those horrible green trousers of hers done up with safety pins, did you notice? She just doesn't care what she looks like. She's an utter mess."

It was true. Edward had to admit it. Yet there was something he liked about Meg, a sort of warm glow, a friendliness. She laughed a lot. The smaller kids loved her.

Meg was young for her age, that was the trouble, a big untidy girl with shaggy brown hair, like an overgrown puppy. She still climbed the trees on the common and rolled down the steep grass bank as he had done when he was a kid. He even saw her playing football with the boys from their old primary school, and had been tempted for a moment to join in. But the ground was wet and muddy, and he was wearing his new trousers. Also his mother was with him.

His mother liked people to look nice. "It only takes a little effort to look clean and tidy," she was fond of telling Edward, "and it makes all the difference to what people think of you. Always remember that, Edward." He knew she didn't approve of Meg. She never said so outright, but he could tell. Her plucked eyebrows always rose when she saw her, and she'd shake her head, as if to say, "Well, really!"

"Isn't that Meg Hunter over there, playing football with those boys?" she'd asked. "Covered in mud, poor girl. Just look at her! It's odd because her mother is really very nice, you know. And the two older girls are always beautifully dressed. You'd never take them for the same family. I wonder Mrs. Hunter lets Meg go around looking like that."

"She's Meg's stepmother," Edward told her.

"It's not always easy being a stepmother," his mother said. "I imagine Meg can be quite a handful."

A Cinderella girl, Edward thought. Poor Meg, nobody cares what she looks like. Perhaps her stepmother grudges every penny she has to spend on her, and won't buy her new clothes or even a hairbrush, so that she has to use safety pins when her zips break and comb her hair with her fingers.

"She's in your class, isn't she?" his mother asked.

"Yes."

"Is she clever?"

"I don't know," Edward said. "I've never noticed."

His mother laughed. "I don't suppose you have," she said. "She's not the sort of girl boys look at."

His mother didn't know everything, however. Edward did look at Meg, quite often. He wasn't certain why. She was plump and her clothes never seemed to fit her and she had big feet. On Sundays, however, when they met by chance in the park, they'd stay together, talking or watching their local team play football. He always looked forward to seeing her.

But it was Bella he really wanted to date. Pretty, popular Bella whom a lot of boys claimed would let you kiss her in the cinema or in the bushes behind the cycle shed. He had never kissed a girl, not properly, and was beginning to feel left out. Of course they might be only boasting.

"Have you ever kissed a girl?" he asked his best friend Michael, who was tall and skinny and clever, and could be trusted not to betray him.

"Of course I have! Millions of times. Can't get away from them," Michael told him. "They swarm over me every Christmas. Mum's only got to put up a bit of mistletoe and I have to hide to avoid being trampled on."

"No, seriously, have you?"

"My lips are sealed," Michael said grandly. "I'm not one to kiss and tell."

"I'm not asking for names. Just a straight answer, yes or no."

"No. What about you."

"No," Edward admitted, "but don't tell anybody."

Michael laughed. "Don't sound so sad. We're still young. Far too young, my mum would say. Do you want to kiss just any girl, or one in particular?"

"I want to kiss Bella Jones."

"Oh, her! I might've guessed. You always want to do what other people do," Michael said. He was not one of Bella's admirers. "Well, why don't you?"

He made it sound easy. Full of hope, Edward had asked Bella to come to see a film with him.

"No, I don't think so," she said.

"Why not?" he asked. "I thought you liked me."

"Whatever gave you that idea?" she said.

"Oh come on! There's a good film on at the Odeon. *Alligator Angel*. I'll treat you. What about tomorrow?"

She shook her head. "Not tomorrow."

"Wednesday?"

"Sorry. Can't manage Wednesday."

"What about Thursday, then?"

"I dunno. I might. I'll think about it," she said.

On Thursday morning, he came to school early, in his new trousers and his best shirt. But when Bella came, she told him she was going out with Kevin Clarke.

"But you promised—"

"I never promised, I just said I might," she told him. "Ask me again sometime."

So he asked her the next day, and the next day, and the next, and every time she said, "I dunno. I might. Ask me again."

The last time she said this, he turned away without a word, and went to look out of the window, ignoring her. She didn't like that.

"What are you looking at?" she asked, coming to stand beside him.

"Nothing in particular."

"Yes, you are. You're looking at Meg Hunter. Here she comes, late as usual. Doesn't she look stupid when she runs? Look at that smudge on her face! She can't have washed at all this morning."

Edward knew how Meg got smudges on her face. Sometimes, when he was late, he saw her going along the road in front of him, trailing her fingers over the ledges of the buildings, stroking the dusty plastic dog outside the pet shop, then pushing her unruly hair back from her face with sooty hands.

"It's only dust," he said.

"And what on earth does she think she's wearing? That cardigan's hideous! And it's coming unraveled at the sleeve. Why doesn't she make her stepmother buy her some decent clothes?"

"What she needs is a fairy godmother, a pumpkin, and a prince," Edward said.

"What she needs is a hot bath and a haircut," Bella retorted, wrinkling her pretty little nose. "Don't tell me you fancy her, Edward?"

Before he could answer, Mr. Dunlock, their teacher, came into the room and ordered them to their places. Edward saw Meg, trying to slip unnoticed into the room, trip over someone's leg—whose? was it Bella's?—and stumble heavily against one of the tables.

"Late again, Meg?" Mr. Dunlock said. He peered at her through his spectacles. "What's that on your face? It looks like soot. Go and wash it off, there's a good girl."

As Meg left the room, some of the girls giggled and whispered. Edward was too far away to see who they were. He wondered if Bella was one of them. She could be spiteful, he'd already found that out, but he didn't want to have to start again with another girl. He was used to being in love with her, used to asking her out, even used to being refused.

There was something to be said for unrequited love. It was safer. Often, in his sleep, when he tried to kiss Bella, he tripped over his own feet and missed her altogether. Once he dreamed he was sitting next to her in the dark cinema, holding her hand. But when he leaned over to kiss her, she suddenly turned into Mrs. Trenter, their head teacher, who shouted angrily, "Edward Walden, you've failed your tests! What will your mother say?"

Nevertheless it hurt his pride that Bella should keep on refusing him when she went out with several other boys who were not, he considered, better looking or more amusing or in any way nicer than he was.

"I don't mean to be conceited, but honestly!" he said to his friend Michael. "She's been out with Kevin a lot, and he's the dregs. Why do you think it is?"

"The girl's daft," Michael said kindly. "She's got bad taste."

The next Sunday, Edward walked moodily in the park, looking for Meg. He found her sitting in her favorite tree and climbed up beside her.

"Do you think there's something wrong with me?" he asked.

"In what way? Have you got a pain or spots or something?"

"No. I meant . . . Am I off-putting in any way? Have I got halitosis or do my feet stink?"

"No," she said.

"If you were Bella, would you rather go out with me or Kevin Clarke?"

Meg laughed. "Kevin Clarke writes her poems," she said.

"Poems?" Edward repeated in astonishment. "Whatever for?"

"She likes them. She sticks them in an album opposite photographs of herself, and shows them to us."

"Good grief," Edward said, appalled by this new slant on his beloved. "What are they about?"

"They're all about her, of course," Meg told him. "You know the sort of thing:

"Oh, Bella's hair is brighter than the sun,
And Bella's eyes are bluer than the sky—"

"What rot!" Edward said in disgust. "It's not even true. Bella's hair is pretty enough, but I bet it's never ripened any tomatoes. I wonder she can stomach such tripe. She must be terribly vain."

Meg didn't say anything.

"*You* wouldn't want anyone to write poems to you, would you, Meg?" he asked.

"I don't know. Just once, perhaps. But nobody ever will," she said. He thought she sounded a bit wistful.

"I'll write you a poem, if you like," he offered. "Not that I'm any good at it, but I bet I can do as well as Kevin. Shall I?"

"Don't say that my hair will ripen tomatoes because it won't," she said, pushing it back from her face and leaving a smudge on her nose. "It might do to plant mustard and cress in. Mum's always trying to persuade me to have it cut."

"I shall be strictly truthful," he promised.

"Oh dear."

After a moment, he began:

> *"You hair is rough and long and needs a cut,*
> *Your eyes are . . ."*

"What color are your eyes, Meg? I can't remember. Look at me, please."

She turned her head. Her eyes were a greenish hazel and very bright. They reminded him of the sea at Cosheston, sparkling over the pebbles in the sunlight . . .

> *"Your mermaid eyes are flecked with gold and green.*
> *Your nose is smudged, your sleeve unraveled but*
> *Of all the girls at school you are my queen."*

He shouldn't have said that last line. It wasn't true, was it? What about Bella? Besides, he couldn't date Meg. His mother would have a fit and everybody at school would tease him. He looked at her anxiously, hoping she wouldn't take it seriously, but she only laughed and told him it was a splendid poem, far better than any of Kevin's.

"Don't worry," she said. "I won't tell Bella."

At the end of term, their school had a summer disco in the assembly hall. Edward didn't think he'd go. He had given up asking Bella to come out with him, and no longer dreamed of her at night. So he was surprised when she came up to him and said, "Aren't you going to ask if you can take me to the summer disco, Edward?"

"You don't need anyone to go with. You can just go," he told her.

"I know that," she said. "I just thought you might want to call for me so we could go together."

He looked at her suspiciously. "Would you come with me if I asked you?"

"I dunno. I might," she said and ran off, giggling.

"And I might ask some other girl," he said, and walked off. He knew whom he was going to ask. It was only when he found Meg in the library that it occurred to him that she might refuse.

"Please," he asked, as she hesitated.

"I thought you'd ask Bella Jones," she said.

"No, I'm asking you."

"I can't dance," she said. "I've never been to a disco."

"Nor have I," he told her and they smiled at one another.

He was nervous, standing outside the school on the Saturday of the party. Sometimes he was afraid Meg would not come after all, and Bella would laugh. Sometimes he was afraid Meg would come in her old green trousers, still done up with a safety pin, with her hair unbrushed and her face smudged, and Bella would laugh even louder. Bella had arrived with Kevin Clarke, and they were waiting in the entrance, looking at him and sniggering; Bella with her yellow hair frizzed out and her claws sharpened.

"Who are you waiting for, Edward?" she called out, but just then a big silver car drew up outside the school gates, and a girl in a sea-green dress got out. Her long brown hair was sleek and shining, earrings sparkled in her ears and there were silver buckles on her shoes. As she walked toward them, the thin material of her dress swirled out like the waves of the sea.

Everyone stared.

"Meg," Edward said, coming forward. "Meg, you look fabulous."

"Don't I look posh? I hardly know myself," she told him, laughing. "Mum and my sisters took me in hand. They've been longing to do it for ages, but I wouldn't let them. Mum's brought me a whole lot of new clothes, Josie gave me these earrings and Netta these bracelets."

She was no Cinderella, after all. She was Meg, whose family loved her, enough to let her play football in the park and climb trees when she wanted to, and to do her proud when the time came. She's beautiful, he thought, and felt for a moment an odd pang of loss. Had she gone for good, the laughing, untidy, romping girl who'd not wanted to grow up?

"Don't change too much," he said. Then, as she looked up at him, he noticed a small smudge of eyeblack on her left cheek. Without thinking, he bent down and kissed her, forgetting that Bella and her friends were watching until he heard the catcalls. He didn't care what they thought, not now. It was as if the kiss had broken a spell and set him free. Nobody was going to tell him what to think any longer, nor choose his friends for him. This was the girl he had always liked. The others could suit themselves.

THE NIGHTINGALE
AND THE ROSE

OSCAR WILDE

"**S**HE SAID THAT she would dance with me if I brought her red roses," cried the young Student, "but in all my garden there is no red rose."

From her nest in the holm-oak tree the Nightingale heard him, and she looked out through the leaves and wondered.

"No red rose in all my garden!" he cried, and his beautiful eyes filled with tears. "Ah, on what little things does happiness depend! I have read all that the wise men have written, and all the secrets of philosophy are mine, yet for want of a red rose is my life made wretched."

"Here at last is a true lover," said the Nightingale. "Night after night have I sung of him though I knew him not: night after night have I told his story to the stars and now I see him. His hair is dark as the hyacinth-blossom, and his lips are red as the rose of his desire, but passion has made his face like pale ivory and sorrow has set her seal upon his brow."

"The Prince gives a ball tomorrow night," murmured the

young Student, "and my love will be of the company. If I bring her a red rose she will dance with me till dawn. If I bring her a red rose, I shall hold her in my arms, and she will lean her head upon my shoulder and her hand will be clasped in mine. But there is no red rose in my garden, so I shall sit lonely and she will pass me by. She will have no heed of me, and my heart will break."

"Here, indeed, is the true lover," said the Nightingale. "What I sing of, he suffers: what is joy to me, to him is pain. Surely love is a wonderful thing. It is more precious than emeralds and dearer than fine opals. Pearls and pomegranates cannot buy it, nor is it set forth in the marketplace. It may not be purchased of the merchants, nor can it be weighed out in the balance for gold."

"The musicians will sit in their gallery," said the young Student, "and play upon their stringed instruments, and my love will dance to the sound of the harp and the violin. She will dance so lightly that her feet will not touch the floor, and the courtiers in their gay dresses will throng round her. But with me she will not dance, for I have no red rose to give her;" and he flung himself down on the grass, and buried his face in his hands, and wept.

"Why is he weeping?" asked a little Green Lizard, as he ran past him with his tail in the air.

"Why, indeed?" said a Butterfly, who was fluttering about after a sunbeam.

"Why, indeed?" whispered a Daisy to his neighbor, in a soft, low voice.

"He is weeping for a red rose," said the Nightingale.

"For a red rose?" they cried; "how very ridiculous!" and the little Lizard, who was something of a cynic, laughed outright.

But the Nightingale understood the secret of the Student's sorrow, and she sat silent in the oak-tree, and thought about the mystery of Love.

Suddenly she spread her brown wings for flight, and soared into the air. She passed through the grove like a shadow and like a shadow she sailed across the garden.

In the center of the grass-plot was standing a beautiful rose-tree, and when she saw it she flew over to it, and lit upon a spray.

"Give me a red rose," she cried, "and I will sing you my sweetest song."

But the Tree shook its head.

"My roses are white," it answered; "as white as the foam of the sea, and whiter than the snow on the mountain. But go to my brother who grows round the old sun-dial, and perhaps he will give you what you want."

So the Nightingale flew over to the Rose-tree that was growing round the old sun-dial.

"Give me a red rose," she cried, "and I will sing you my sweetest song."

But the Tree shook its head.

"My roses are yellow," it answered; "as yellow as the hair of the mermaiden who sits upon an amber throne, and yellower than the daffodil that blooms in the meadow before the mower comes with his scythe. But go to my brother who grows beneath the Student's window, and perhaps he will give you what you want."

So the Nightingale flew over to the Rose-tree that was growing beneath the Student's window.

"Give me a red rose," she cried, "and I will sing you my sweetest song."

But the Tree shook its head.

"My roses are red," it answered; "as red as the feet of the dove, and redder than the great fans of coral that wave and wave in the ocean-cavern. But the winter has chilled my veins, and the frost has nipped my buds, and the storm has broken my branches, and I shall have no roses at all this year."

"One red rose is all I want," cried the Nightingale, "only one red rose! Is there no way by which I can get it?"

"There is a way," answered the Tree; "but it is so terrible that I dare not tell it to you."

"Tell it to me," said the Nightingale, "I am not afraid."

"If you want a red rose," said the Tree, "you must build it out of music by moonlight, and stain it with your own heart's-blood. You must sing to me with your breast against a thorn. All night long you must sing to me, and the thorn must pierce your heart, and your life-blood must flow into my veins, and become mine."

"Death is a great price to pay for a red rose," cried the Nightingale, "and Life is very dear to all. It is pleasant to sit in the green wood, and to watch the Sun in his chariot of gold, and the Moon in her chariot of pearl. Sweet is the scent of the hawthorn, and sweet are the bluebells that hide in the valley, and the heather that blows on the hill. Yet Love is better than Life, and what is the heart of a bird compared to the heart of a man?"

So she spread her brown wings for flight, and soared into the air. She swept over the garden like a shadow, and like a shadow she sailed through the grove.

The young Student was still lying on the grass, where she had left him, and the tears were not yet dry in his beautiful eyes.

"Be happy," cried the Nightingale, "be happy; you shall have your red rose. I will build it out of music by moonlight, and stain it with my own heart's-blood. All that I ask of you in return is that you will be a true lover, for Love is wiser than Philosophy, though he is wise, and mightier than Power, though he is mighty. Flame-colored are his wings, and colored like flame is his body. His lips are sweet as honey, and his breath is like frankincense."

The Student looked up from the grass, and listened, but he could not understand what the Nightingale was saying to him, for he only knew the things that are written down in books.

But the Oak-tree understood, and felt sad, for he was very fond of the little Nightingale who had built her nest in his branches.

"Sing me one last song," he whispered; "I shall feel

lonely when you are gone."

So the Nightingale sang to the Oak-tree, and her voice was like water bubbling from a silver jar.

When she had finished her song, the Student got up, and pulled a notebook and a lead-pencil out of his pocket.

"She has form," he said to himself, as he walked away through the grove—"that cannot be denied to her; but has she got feeling? I am afraid not. In fact, she is like most artists; she is all style without any sincerity. She would not sacrifice herself for others. She thinks merely of music, and everybody knows that the arts are selfish. Still it must be admitted that she has some beautiful notes in her voice. What a pity it is that they do not mean anything, or do any practical good!" And he went into his room, and lay down on his little pallet-bed, and began to think of his love; and, after a time, he fell asleep.

And when the moon shone in the heavens the Nightingale flew to the Rose-tree, and set her breast against the thorn. All night long she sang, with her breast against the thorn, and the cold crystal Moon leaned down and listened. All night long she sang, and the thorn went deeper and deeper into her breast, and her life-blood ebbed away from her.

She sang first of the birth of love in the heart of a boy and a girl. And on the topmost spray of the Rose-tree there blossomed a marvelous rose, petal following petal, as song followed song. Pale was it, at first, as the mist that hangs over the river—pale as the feet of the morning, and silver as the wings of the dawn. As the shadow of a rose in a mirror of silver, as the shadow of a rose in a water-pool, so was the rose that blossomed on the topmost spray of the Tree.

But the Tree cried to the Nightingale to press closer against the thorn. "Press closer, little Nightingale," cried the Tree, "or the Day will come before the rose is finished."

So the Nightingale pressed closer against the thorn, and louder and louder grew her song, for she sang of the birth

44

of passion in the soul of a man and a maid.

And a delicate flush of pink came into the leaves of the rose, like the flush in the face of the bridegroom when he kisses the lips of the bride. But the thorn had not yet reached her heart, so the rose's heart remained white, for only a Nightingale's heart's-blood can crimson the heart of a rose.

And the Tree cried to the Nightingale to press closer against the thorn. "Press closer, little Nightingale," cried the Tree, "or the Day will come before the rose is finished."

So the Nightingale pressed closer against the thorn, and the thorn touched her heart, and a fierce pang of pain shot through her. Bitter, bitter was the pain, and wilder and wilder grew her song, for she sang of the Love that is perfected by Death, of the Love that dies not in the tomb.

And the marvelous rose became crimson, like the rose of the eastern sky. Crimson was the girdle of petals, and crimson as a ruby was the heart.

But the Nightingale's voice grew fainter, and her little wings began to beat, and a film came over her eyes. Fainter and fainter grew her song, and she felt something choking in her throat.

Then she gave one last burst of music. The white Moon heard it, and she forgot the dawn, and lingered on in the sky. The red rose heard it, and it trembled all over with ecstasy, and opened its petals to the cold morning air. Echo bore it to her purple cavern in the hills and woke the sleeping shepherds from their dreams. It floated through the reeds of the river, and they carried its message to the sea.

"Look, look!" cried the Tree, "the rose is finished now;" but the Nightingale made no answer, for she was lying dead in the long grass, with the thorn in her heart.

And at noon the Student opened his window and looked out.

"Why, what a wonderful piece of luck!" he cried; "here is a red rose! I have never seen any rose like it in all my life. It is so beautiful that I am sure it has a long Latin name;" and he leaned down and plucked it.

Then he put on his hat, and ran up to the Professor's house with the rose in his hand.

The daughter of the Professor was sitting in the doorway winding blue silk on a reel, and her little dog was lying at her feet.

"You said that you would dance with me if I brought you a red rose," cried the Student. "Here is the reddest rose in all the world. You will wear it tonight next your heart, and as we dance together it will tell you how I love you."

But the girl frowned.

"I am afraid it will not go with my dress," she answered; "and, besides, the Chamberlain's nephew has sent me some real jewels, and everybody knows that jewels cost far more than flowers."

"Well, upon my word, you are very ungrateful," said the Student angrily; and he threw the rose into the street, where it fell into the gutter, and a cart-wheel went over it.

"Ungrateful!" said the girl. "I tell you what, you are very rude; and, after all, who are you? Only a Student. Why, I don't believe you have even got silver buckles to your shoes as the Chamberlain's nephew has;" and she got up from her chair and went into the house.

"What a silly thing Love is!" said the Student as he walked away. "It is not half as useful as Logic, for it does not prove anything, and it is always telling one of things that are not going to happen, and making one believe things that are not true. In fact, it is quite unpractical, and, as in this age to be practical is everything, I shall go back to Philosophy and study Metaphysics."

So he returned to his room and pulled out a great dusty book, and began to read.

LOVE LETTERS

KATE WALKER

MY NAME'S NICK and my chick's name's Fleur. And she has a friend called Helen who's got a boyfriend named Clive. Now this Clive is really weird. Well, he does one weird thing I know of anyway: he writes three-page letters to his girlfriend, Helen, *every* day.

"What's wrong with the nerd?" I asked Fleur. She'd spent a whole lunch time telling me about him.

"There's nothing *wrong* with him," she said. "You're so unromantic, Nick."

"Of course I'm not unromantic!" I said, and I offered her a lick of my ice cream to prove it. She groaned and pulled her P.E. bag over her head. She didn't want to talk to me anymore.

When girls go quiet, that's a bad sign!

"What's wrong?" I asked her.

"You don't love me," she said.

"Of course I love you," I told her. I offered her my whole ice cream. She wouldn't take it.

"You don't love me *enough*," she said.

"How much is *enough*?"

How much ice cream did it take?

"You don't write *me* letters like Clive does to Helen," she said.

"I don't need to, I see you every day in Computers," I said. "*And* Chemistry."

"Clive sees Helen every day in Biology, and Textiles, and Home Science, and assembly, and roll call," she said, "and he writes letters to *her*!"

I knew what was happening here: my girlfriend was cooling on me.

"OK," I said, "I'll write you a letter."

"Aw, Nick!" She whipped her P.E. bag off her head.

I was glad I'd weakened. Fleur is really gorgeous. I couldn't risk losing her for the sake of a few lines scrawled on a piece of paper. I'm the envy of the boys' locker room, having her for a girlfriend.

I sat down that night and began my first letter: "Dear Fleur . . ." Then I stared at the page for the next half hour. What do you write in letters to someone you see every day? I chewed my pencil; I chewed my nails. Then, in desperation, I finally asked Mum.

"Write about the things you have in common," Mum said, so I wrote the following: "Wasn't that computer class on Tuesday a ROAR? The best bit was when Brando tilted the computer to show us the little button underneath and the monitor fell off."

I wrote about the Chemistry class too, though it wasn't quite as interesting. Not a single kid muffed their experiment and blew their eyebrows off. But then I got really creative at the end of the letter and added a postscript written in Basic.

I got the letter back next day with "five-and-a-half out of twenty" marked on the bottom.

"What was wrong with it?" I asked Fleur.

"You made a lot of spelling mistakes for one thing," she said.

"I was being *myself*!" I told her.

"I didn't notice," she said. "You didn't say anything *personal* in it!"

Is that what she wanted, a *personal* letter?

I thought it over for five minutes. There were guys all round the lunch area just waiting to take my place and share their chocolate milk with the fabulous Fleur. If revealing a few personal secrets was what it took to keep her, I could do it.

"Dear Fleur . . ." I began the second letter that night. "This is not something I'd tell everyone, but I use a deodorant. Only on sports days or in really hot weather of course."

No, that was too personal. I ripped up the page and started again. "Dear Fleur, Guess what? Mrs. Hessel blew me up in History today for no reason at all. I was embarrassed to death. Goggle-eyes Gilda laughed her stupid head off."

Actually, once I'd got started I found the personal stuff not that hard to write. I told Fleur what mark I'd *really* got in the English half-yearlies. Then I told her about a movie I'd seen where this pioneer farming guy loses his plow horse, then loses his wife, then his children, and then his cows get hoof rot. But even though he sits down and bawls his eyes out about it, in the end he walks off into the sunset, a stronger man.

"I'd like to suffer a great personal loss like that," I told Fleur in the letter, "and walk away stronger and nobler for it."

Her sole comment on letter number two was: "You didn't say anything in it about *me*." And she went off to eat lunch with Helen.

It was time to hit the panic button. Fleur was "drifting." I stuffed my sandwiches back in my bag and went looking for Clive. I bailed him up under the stairwell.

"OK, what do you put in your letters to Helen?" I asked him.

Clive turned out to be a decent kid. He not only told me, he gave me a photocopy of the latest letter he was writing to Helen.

You should have seen it!

"Darling Helen, Your hair is like gold. Your eyes remind me of twilight reflected on Throsby Creek. Your ear lobes are . . . Your eyelashes are . . ." And so on. It was what you'd call a poetic autopsy.

And as if that wasn't bad enough, he then got into the declarations of love: "You're special to me because . . . I yearn for you in History because . . . I can't eat noodles without thinking of you because . . ."

"Do girls really go for this sort of thing?" I asked him.

"Helen does," he said. "She'd drop me tomorrow if I stopped writing her letters. It's the price you pay if you want to keep your girlfriend."

So I began my third letter, with Clive's photocopy propped up in front of me as a guide.

"Dear Fleur, Your hair is like . . ." I began.

Actually, I'd always thought it was like cotton candy, pretty from a distance but all gooey when you touched it—too much hair spray, I suppose.

I scrapped that opening and started again.

"Dear Fleur, Your eyes are like . . ."

Actually, they're a bit small and squinty. I think she might need glasses but she's not letting on.

Scrub the eyes.

"Dear Fleur, Your face is excellent overall. You look like one of those soap-opera dolls."

I thought I would've been able to go on for hours about her face, but having said that, it seemed to sum her up.

I moved on to the declarations: "I love you because . . ." I chewed my pencil again, then my fingernails. This time I couldn't ask Mum.

Why did I love Fleur? Because she was spunky. Because all the guys thought so too. Well, not all of them. Some of them thought she wasn't all that interesting to talk to, but I put that down to jealousy.

Still, I began to wonder, what *had* we talked about in the three weeks we'd been going together? Not much really. She'd never been interested enough in my hockey playing to ask in-depth questions about it. And, I have to admit, I hadn't found her conversation on white ankle boots all that riveting either.

No wonder I was having so much trouble writing letters to her. We had nothing in common. I barely knew her. What were her views on nuclear disarmament? Maybe she didn't have any. Was she pro-Libyan? I didn't know.

I scrapped the letter, scrapped Clive's photocopy, and started again, this time with no trouble at all.

"Dear Fleur, This writing of letters was a very good idea because it gives me the opportunity to say something important to you. I think you're a nice girl and I've enjoyed going steady with you for three weeks but I think we should call it off. Even if it's a great personal loss to both of us, I'm sure we'll walk away stronger and nobler. Yours sincerely, Nick."

I slipped the letter to her in Computers. She didn't take it too badly, just ripped it up and fed it through the shredder. But then two days later photocopies of my *personal* letter started to circulate the school.

I didn't mind, though, because as a result of that, Goggle-eyes Gilda slipped me a note in History that said, briefly: "I like your style, Nick. You've got depth." I took another look at Goggle-eyes. I didn't mind her style either. She has this terrific laugh and she's a whiz on computers.

I wrote back straightaway, my own kind of letter this time—honest and to the point: "Dear Gilda, That three-minute talk you gave on speech day about Third World Famine Relief was really excellent. I'll be eating lunch in the quad if you'd care to join me."

THE GIRL WHO
LOVED THE SUN

DIANA WYNNE JONES

THERE WAS A GIRL called Phega who became a tree.
Stories from the ancient times when Phega lived
would have it that when women turned into trees it
was always under duress, because a god was pursuing
them, but Phega turned into a tree voluntarily. She did it
from the moment she entered her teens. It was not easy and
it took a deal of practice, but she kept at it. She would go
into the fields beyond the manor house where she lived
and there she would put down roots, spread her arms, and
say, "For you I shall spread out my arms." Then she would
become a tree.

She did this because she was in love with the sun. The
people who looked after her when she was a child told her
that the sun loved the trees above all other living things.
Phega concluded that this must be so from the way most
trees shed their leaves in winter when the sun was unable
to attend to them very much. As Phega could not
remember a time when the sun had not been more to her

54

than mother, father or life itself, it followed that she had to become a tree.

At first she was not a very good tree. The trunk of her tended to bulge at hips and breast and was usually an improbable brown color. The largest number of branches she could achieve was four or five at the most. These stood out at unconvincing angles and grew large pallid leaves in a variety of shapes. She strove with these defects valiantly, but for a long time it always seemed that when she got her trunk to look more natural, her branches were fewer and more misshapen, and when she grew halfway decent branches, either her trunk relapsed or her leaves were too large or too yellow.

"Oh, sun," she sighed, "do help me to be more pleasing to you." Yet it seemed unlikely that the sun was even attending to her. "But he will!" Phega said and, driven by hope and yearning, she continued to stand in the field, striving to spread out more plausible branches. Whatever shape they were, she could still revel in the sun's impartial warmth on them and in the searching strength of her roots reaching into the earth. Whether the sun was attending or not, she knew the deep peace of a tree's long, wordless thoughts. The rain was pure delight to her, instead of the necessary evil it was to other people, and the dew was a marvel.

The following spring, to her delight, she achieved a reasonable shape, with a narrow, lissome trunk and a cloud of spread branches, not unlike a fruiting tree. "Look at me, sun," she said. "Is this the kind of tree you like?"

The sun glanced down at her. She stood still as the instant between hope and despair. It seemed that he attended to the wordless words.

But the sun passed on beaming, not unkindly, to glance at the real apple trees that stood on the slope of the hill.

"I need to be different in some way," Phega said to herself.

She became a girl again and studied the apple trees. She

watched them put out big pale buds and saw how the sun drew those buds open to become leaves and white flowers. Choking with the hurt of rejection, she saw the sun dwelling lovingly on those flowers, which made her think at first that flowers were what she needed. Then she saw that the sun drew those flowers on, quite ruthlessly, until they died, and that what came after were green blobs that turned into apples.

"Now I know what I need," she said.

It took a deal of hard work, but the following spring she was able to say, "Look at me, sun. For you I shall hold out my arms budded with growing things," and spread branches full of white blossom that she was prepared to force on into fruit.

This time, however, the sun's gaze fell on her only in the way it fell on all living things. She was very dejected. Her yearning for the sun to love her grew worse.

"I still need to be different in some way," she said.

That year she studied the sun's ways and likings as she had never studied them before. In between she was a tree. Her yearning for the sun had grown so great that when she was in human form, it was as if she were less than half alive. Her parents and other human company were shadowy to her. Only when she was a tree with her arms spread to the sunlight did she feel she was truly in existence.

As that year took its course she noticed that the place the sun first touched unfailingly in the morning was the top of the hill beyond the apple trees. And it was the place where he lingered last at sunset. Phega saw this must be the place the sun loved best. So, though it was twice as far from the manor, Phega went daily to the top of that hill and took root there. This meant that she had an hour more of the sun's warm company to spread her boughs into, but the situation was not otherwise as good as the fields. The top of the hill was very dry. When she put down roots, the soil was thin and tasted peculiar. And there was always a wind up there. Phega found she grew bent over and rather stunted.

"But what more can I do?" she said to the sun. "For you I shall spread out my arms, budded with growing things, and root within the ground you warm, accepting what that brings."

The sun gave no sign of having heard, although he continued to linger on the top of the hill at the beginning and end of each day. Phega would walk home in the twilight considering how she might grow roots that were adapted to the thin soil and pondering ways and means to strengthen her trunk against the wind. She walked slightly bent over and her skin was pale and withered.

Up till now Phega's parents had indulged her and not interfered. Her mother said, "She's very young." Her father agreed and said, "She'll get over this obsession with rooting herself in time." But when they saw her looking pale and withered and walking with a stoop, they felt the time had come to intervene. They said to one another, "She's old enough to marry now and she's ruining her looks."

The next day they stopped Phega before she left the manor on her way to the hill. "You must give up this pining and rooting," her mother said to her. "No girl ever found a husband by being out in all weathers like this."

And her father said, "I don't know what you're after with this tree nonsense. I mean, we can all see you're very good at it, but it hasn't got much bearing on the rest of life, has it? You're our only child, Phega. You have the future of the manor to consider. I want you married to the kind of man I can trust to look after the place when I'm gone. That's not the kind of man who's going to want to marry a tree."

Phega burst into tears and fled away across the fields and up the hill.

"Oh, dear!" her father said guiltily. "Did I go too far?"

"Not at all," said her mother. "I would have said it if you hadn't. We must start looking for a husband for her. Find the right man and this nonsense will slide out of her head the moment she claps eyes on him."

It happened that Phega's father had to go away on business anyway. He agreed to extend his journey and look for a suitable husband for Phega while he was away. His wife gave him a good deal of advice on the subject, ending with a very strong directive not to tell any prospective suitor that Phega had this odd habit of becoming a tree—at least not until the young man was safely proved to be interested in marriage anyway. And as soon as her husband was away from the manor, she called two servants she could trust and told them to follow Phega and watch how she turned into a tree. "For it must be a process we can put a stop to somehow," she said, "and if you can find out how we can stop her for good, so much the better."

Phega, meanwhile, rooted herself breathlessly into the shallow soil at the top of the hill. "Help me," she called out to the sun. "They're talking of marrying me and the only one I love is you!"

The sun pushed aside an intervening cloud and

considered her with astonishment. "Is this why you so continually turn into a tree?" he said.

Phega was too desperate to consider the wonder of actually, at last, talking to the sun. She said, "All I do, I do in the remote, tiny hope of pleasing you and causing you to love me as I love you."

"I had no idea," said the sun and he added, not unkindly, "but I do love everything according to its nature, and your nature is human. I might admire you for so skillfully becoming a tree, but that is, when all is said and done, only an imitation of a tree. It follows that I love you better as a human." He beamed and was clearly about to pass on.

Phega threw herself down on the ground, half woman and half tree, and wept bitterly, thrashing her branches and rolling back and forth. "But I love you," she cried out. "You are the light of the world and I love you. I *have* to be a tree because then I have no heart to ache for you, and even as a tree I ache at night because you aren't there. Tell me what I can do to make you love me."

The sun paused. "I do not understand your passion," he said. "I have no wish to hurt you, but this is the truth: I cannot love you as an imitation of a tree."

A small hope came to Phega. She raised the branches of her head. "Could you love me if I stopped pretending to be a tree?"

"Naturally," said the sun, thinking this would appease her. "I would love you according to your nature, human woman."

59

"Then I make a bargain with you," said Phega. "I will stop pretending and you will love me."

"If that is what you want," said the sun and went on his way.

Phega shook her head free of branches and her feet from the ground and sat up, brooding, with her chin on her hands. That was how her mother's servants found her and watched her warily from among the apple trees. She sat there for hours. She had bargained with the sun as a person might bargain for their very life, out of the desperation of her love, and she needed to work out a plan to back her bargain with. It gave her slight shame that she was trying to trap such a being as the sun, but she knew that was not going to stop her. She was beyond shame.

"There is no point imitating something that already exists," she said to herself, "because that is pretending to be that thing. I will have to be some kind that is totally new."

Phega came down from the hill and studied trees again. Because of the hope her bargain had given her, she studied in a new way, with passion and depth, all the time her father was away. She ranged far afield to the forests in the valleys beyond the manor, where she spent days among the trees, standing still as a tree, but in human shape—which puzzled her mother's servants exceedingly—listening to the creak of their growth and every rustle of every leaf, until she knew them as trees knew other trees and comprehended the abiding restless stillness of them. The entire shape of a tree against the sky became open to her and she came to know all their properties. Trees had power. Willows had pithy centers and grew fast; they caused sleep. Elder was pithy too; it could give powerful protection, but had a touchy nature and should be treated politely. But the oak and the ash, the giant trees that held their branches closest to the sun's love, had the greatest power of all. Oak was constancy and ash was change. Phega studied these two longest and most respectfully.

"I need the properties of both these," she said.

She carried away branches of leafing twigs to study as she walked home, noting the join of twig to twig and the way the leaves were fastened on. Evergreens impressed her by the way they kept leaves for the sun even in winter, but she was soon sure they did it out of primitive parsimony. Oaks, on the other hand, had their leaves tightly knotted on by reason of their strength.

"I shall need the same kind of strength," Phega said.

As autumn drew on, the fruiting trees preoccupied her, since it was clear that it was growth and fruition the sun seemed most to love. They all, she saw, partook of the natures of both oaks and elders, even hawthorn, rowan and hazel. Indeed many of them were related to the lowlier bushes and fruiting plants; but the giant trees that the sun most loved were more exclusive in their pedigrees.

"Then I shall be like the oak," Phega said, "but bear better fruit."

Winter approached and trees were felled for firewood. Phega was there, where the foresters were working, anxiously inspecting the rings of the sawn trunk and interrogating the very sawdust. This mystified the servants who were following her. They asked the foresters if they had any idea what Phega was doing.

The foresters shook their heads and said, "She is not quite sane, but we know she is very wise."

The servants had to be content with this. At least after that they had an easier time, for Phega was mostly at home in the manor examining the texture of the logs for the fires. She studied the bark on the outside and then the longwise grains and the roundwise rings of the interior, and she came to an important conclusion: an animal stopped growing when it had attained a certain shape, but a tree did not.

"I see now," she said, "that I have by no means finished growing." And she was very impatient because winter had put a stop to all growth, so that she had to wait for spring to study its nature.

In the middle of winter her father came home. He had found the perfect husband for Phega and was anxious to tell Phega and her mother all about the man. This man was a younger son of a powerful family, he said, and he had been a soldier for some years, during which time he had distinguished himself considerably and gained a name for sense and steadiness. Now he was looking for a wife to marry and settle down with. Though he was not rich, he was not poor either and he was on good terms with the wealthier members of his family. It was, said Phega's father, a most desirable match.

Phega barely listened to all this. She went away to look at the latest load of logs before her father had finished speaking. "He may not ever come here," she said to herself, "and if he does, he will see I am not interested and go away again."

"Did I say something wrong?" her father asked her

mother. "I had hoped to show her that the man has advantages that far outweigh the fact that he is not in his first youth."

"No—it's just the way she is," said Phega's mother. "Have you invited the man here?"

"Yes, he is coming in the spring," her father said. "His name is Evor. Phega will like him."

Phega's mother was not entirely too sure of this. She called the servants she had set to follow Phega to her privately and asked them what they had found out. "Nothing," they said. "We think she has given up turning into a tree. She has never so much as put forth a root while we are watching her."

"I hope you are right," said Phega's mother. "But I want you to go on watching her, even more carefully than before. It is now extremely important that we know how to stop her becoming a tree if she ever threatens to do so."

The servants sighed, knowing they were in for another dull and difficult time. And they were not mistaken because, as soon as the first snowdrops appeared, Phega was out in the countryside studying the way things grew. As far as the servants were concerned, she would do nothing but sit or stand for hours watching a bud, or a tree, or a nest of mice or birds. As far as Phega was concerned, it was a long fascination as she divined how cells multiplied again and again and at length discovered that, while animals took food from solid things, plants took their main food from the sun himself. "I think that may be the secret at last," she said.

This puzzled the servants, but they reported it to Phega's mother all the same. Her answer was, "I *thought* so. Be ready to bring her home the instant she shows a root or a shoot."

The servants promised to do this, but Phega was not ready yet. She was busy watching the whole course of spring growth transform the forest. So it happened that Evor arrived to meet his prospective bride and Phega was not there. She had not even noticed that everyone in the manor was preparing a feast in Evor's honor. Her parents sent messengers to the forest to fetch her, while Evor first kicked his heels for several hours in the hall and finally, to their embarrassment, grew impatient and went out into the yard. There he wondered whether to order his horse and leave.

"I conclude from this delay," he said to himself, "that the girl is not willing—and one thing I do not want is a wife I have to force." Nevertheless, he did not order his horse. Though Phega's parents had been at pains to keep from him any suggestion that Phega was not as other girls were, he had been unable to avoid hearing rumors on the way. For by this time Phega's fame was considerable. The first gossip he heard, when he was farthest away, was that his prospective bride was a witch. This he had taken for

envious persons' way of describing wisdom and pressed on. As he came nearer, rumor had it that she was very wise, and he felt justified—though the latest rumor he had heard, when he was no more than ten miles from the manor, was that Phega was at least a trifle mad. But each rumor came accompanied by statements about Phega's appearance which were enough to make him tell himself that it was too late to turn back anyway. This kept him loitering in the yard. He wanted to set eyes on her himself.

He was still waiting when Phega arrived, walking in through the gate quickly but rather pensively. It was a gray day, with the sun hidden, and she was sad. "But," she told herself, "I may as well see this suitor and tell him there was no point in his coming and get it over with." She knew her parents were responsible and did not blame the man at all.

Evor looked at her as she came and knew that rumor had understated her looks. The time Phega had spent studying had improved her health and brought her from girl to young woman. She was beautiful. Evor saw that her hair was the color of beer when you hold a glass of it to the light. She was wearing a dress of smooth silver-gray material which showed that her body under it when she moved was smooth-muscled and sturdy—and he liked sturdy women. Her overgarment was a curious light, bright green and floated away from her arms, revealing them to be very round and white. When he looked at her face, which was both round and long, he saw beauty there, but he also saw that she was very wise. Her eyes were gray. He saw a wildness there contained by the deep calm of long, long thought and a capacity to drink in knowledge. He was awed. He was lost.

Phega, for her part, tore her thoughts from many hours of standing longing among the great trees and saw a wiry man of slightly over middle height, who had a bold face with a keen stare to it. She saw he was not young. There was gray to his beard—which always grew more sparsely than he would have liked, though he had combed it carefully for the occasion—and some gray in his hair too. She noticed his hair particularly because he had come to the manor in light armor, to show his status as a soldier and a commander, but he was carrying his helmet politely in the crook of his arm. His intention was to show himself as a polished man of the world. But Phega saw him as iron-colored all over. He made her think of an axe, except that he seemed to have such a lot of hair. She feared he was brutal.

Evor said, "My lady!" and added as a very awkward afterthought, "I came to marry you." As soon as he had said this, it struck him as so wrong and presumptuous a thing to say to a woman like this one, that he hung his head and stared at her feet, which were bare and, though beautiful, stained green with the grass she had walked through. The sight gave him courage. He thought that those feet were human after all, so it followed that the rest of her was, and he looked up at her eyes again. "What a thing to say!" he said.

He smiled in a flustered way. Phega saw that he was somewhat snaggletoothed, not to speak of highly diffident in spite of his gray and military appearance, and possibly in awe of her. She could not see how he could be in awe of her, but his uneven teeth made him a person to her. Of a sudden, he was not just the man her parents had procured for her to marry, but another person like her, with feelings like Phega had herself. "Good gods!" she thought, in considerable surprise. "This is a person I could maybe love after all, if it were not for the sun." And she told him politely that he was very welcome.

They went indoors together and presently sat down to the feast. There Evor got over his awe a little, enough to attempt to talk to Phega. And Phega, knowing he had feelings to be hurt, answered the questions he asked and asked things in return. The result was that before long, to the extreme delight of Phega's parents, they were talking of his time at war and of her knowledge, and laughing together as if they were friends—old friends.

Evor's wonder and joy grew. Long before the feast was over, he knew he could never love any other woman now. The effect of Phega on him was like a physical tie, half-glorious, half-painful, that bound him to respond to every tiny movement of her hand and every flicker of her lashes.

Phega found—and her surprise increased—that she was comfortable with Evor. But however amicably they talked, it was still as if she was only half-alive in the sun's absence —though it was an easy half life—and, as the evening wore on, she felt increasingly confined and trapped. At first she assumed that this feeling was simply due to her having spent so much of the past year out-of-doors. She was so used to having nothing but the sky with the sun in it over her head that she often did find the manor roof confining. But now it was like a cage over her head. And she realized that her growing liking for Evor was causing it.

"If I don't take care," she said to herself, "I shall forget the bargain I made with the sun and drift into this human contract. It is almost too late already. I must act at once."

Thinking this, she said her good nights and went away to sleep.

Evor remained, talking jubilantly with Phega's parents. "When I first saw her," he said, "I thought things were hopeless. But now I think I have a chance. I think she likes me."

Phega's father agreed, but Phega's mother said, "I'm sure she *likes* you all right, but—I caught a look in her eye—this may not be enough to make her marry you."

Saying this, Phega's mother touched on something Evor had sensed and feared himself. His jubilation turned ashy—indeed he felt as if the whole world had been taken by drought: there was no moisture or virtue in it anywhere from pole to pole. "What more can I do?" he said, low and slow.

"Let me tell you something," said Phega's mother.

"Yes," Phega's father broke in eagerly. "Our daughter has a strange habit of—"

"She is," Phega's mother interrupted swiftly, "under an enchantment which we are helpless to break. Only a man who truly loves her can break it."

Hope rose in Evor, as violent as Phega's hope when she bargained with the sun. "Tell me what to do," he said.

Phega's mother considered all the reports her servants had brought her. So far as she knew, Phega had never once turned into a tree all the time her father was away. It was possible she had lost the art. This meant that, with luck, Evor need never know the exact nature of her daughter's eccentricity. "Sometime soon," she said, "probably at dawn, my daughter will be compelled by the enchantment to leave the manor. She will go to the forest or the hill. She may be compelled to murmur words to herself. You must follow her when she goes and, as soon as you see her standing still, you must take her in your arms and kiss her. In this way you will break the spell and she will become your faithful wife ever after." And, Phega's mother told herself, this was very likely what would happen. "For," she thought, "as soon as he kisses her, my daughter will discover that there are certain pleasures to be had from behaving naturally. Then we can all be comfortable again."

"I shall do exactly what you say," said Evor, and he was so uplifted with hope and gratitude that his face was nearly handsome.

All that night he kept watch. He could not have slept anyway. Love roared in his ears and longing choked him. He went over and over the things Phega had said and each individual beauty of her face and body as she said these things, and when, in the dawn, he saw her stealing through the hall to the door, there was a moment when he could not move. She was even more lovely than he remembered.

Phega softly unbarred the door and crossed the yard to unbar the gate. Evor pulled himself together and followed. They walked out across the fields in the white time before sunrise, Phega pacing very upright, with her eyes on the sky where the sun would appear, and Evor stealing after.

He softly took off his armor piece by piece as he followed her and laid it down carefully in case it should clatter and alarm her.

Up the hill Phega went where she stood like one entranced, watching the gold rim of the sun come up. And such was Evor's awe that he loitered a little in the apple trees, admiring her as she stood.

"Now," Phega said, "I have come to fulfill my bargain, Sun, since I fear this is the last time I shall truly want to."

What she did then, she had given much thought to. It was not the way she had been accustomed to turn into a tree before. It was far more thorough. First she put down careful roots, driving each of her toes downward and outward and then forcing them into a network of fleshy cables to make the most of the thin soil at the top of the hill. "Here," she said, "I root within the soil you warm."

Evor saw the ground rise and writhe and low branches grow from her insteps to bury themselves also. "Oh, no!" he cried out. "Your feet were beautiful as they were!" And he began to climb the hill toward her.

Phega frowned, concentrating on the intricacy of feathery rootlets. "But they were not the way I wanted them," she said and she wondered vaguely why he was there. But by then she was putting forth her greatest effort, which left her little attention to spare. Slowly, once her roots were established, she began to coat them with bark before insects could damage them. At the same time, she set to work on her trunk, growing swiftly, grain by growing grain. "Increased by yearly rings," she murmured.

As Evor advanced, he saw her body elongate, coating itself with matte pewter-colored bark as it grew, until he could barely pick out the outline of limbs and muscles inside it. It was like watching a death. "Don't!" he said. "Why are you *doing* this? You were lovely before!"

"I was like all human women," Phega answered, resting before her next great effort. "But when I am finished I shall be a wholly new kind of tree." Having said that, she turned

her attention to the next stage, which she was expecting to enjoy. Now she stretched up her arms, and the hair of her head, yearning into the warmth of the climbing sun, and made it all into limblike boughs which she coated like the rest of her, carefully, with dark silver bark. "For you I shall hold out my arms," she said.

Evor saw her, tree-shaped and twice as tall as himself, and cried out, "Stop!" He was afraid to touch her in this condition. He knelt at her roots in despair.

"I can't stop now," Phega told him gently. She was gathering herself for her final effort and her mind was on that, though the tears she heard breaking his voice did trouble her a little. She put that trouble out of her head. This was the difficult part. She had already elongated every large artery of her body, to pass through her roots and up her trunk and into her boughs. Now she concentrated on lifting her veins, and every nerve with them, without disturbing the rest, out to the ends of her branches, out and up, up and out, into a mass of living twigs, fine-growing and close as her own hair. It was impossible. It hurt—she had not thought it would hurt so much—but she was lifting, tearing her veins, thrusting her nerve ends with them, first into the innumerable fine twigs, then into further particles to make long sharp buds.

Evor looked up as he crouched and saw the great tree surging and thrashing above him. He was appalled at the effort. In the face of this gigantic undertaking he knew he was lost and forgotten and, besides, it was presumptuous to interfere with such willing agony. He saw her strive and strive again to force those sharp buds open. "If you must be a tree," he shouted above the din of her lashing branches, "take me with you somehow, at least!"

"Why should you want that?" Phega asked with wooden lips that had not yet quite closed, just where her main boughs parted.

Evor at last dared to clasp the trunk with its vestigial limbs showing. He shed tears on the gray bark. "Because I

72

love you. I want to be with you."

Trying to see him forced her buds to unfurl, because that was where her senses now were. They spread with myriad shrill agonies, like teeth cutting, and she thought it had killed her, even while she was forcing further nerves and veins to the undersides of all her pale viridian leaves. When it was done, she was all alive and raw in the small hairs on the undersides of those leaves and in the symmetrical ribs of vein on the shiny upper sides, but she could sense Evor crouching at her roots now. She was grateful to him for forcing her to the necessary pain. Her agony responded to his. He was a friend. He had talked of love, and she understood that. She retained just enough of the strength it had taken to change to alter him too to some extent, though not enough to bring him beyond the animal kingdom. The last of her strength was reserved for putting forth small pear-shaped fruit covered with wiry hairs, each containing four triangular nuts. Then, before the wooden gap that was her mouth had entirely closed, she murmured, "Budding with growing things."

She rested for a while, letting the sun harden her leaves to a dark shiny green and ripen her fruit a little. Then she cried wordlessly to the sun, "Look! Remember our bargain. I am an entirely new kind of tree—as strong as an oak, but I bear fruit that everything can eat. Love me. Love me now!" Proudly she shed some of her three-cornered nuts onto the hilltop.

"I see you," said the sun. "This is a lovely tree, but I am not sure what you expect me to do with you."

"Love me!" she cried.

"I do," said the sun. "There is no change in me. The only difference is that I now feed you more directly than I feed that animal at your feet. It is the way I feed all trees. There is nothing else I can do."

Phega knew the sun was right and that her bargain had been her own illusion. It was very bitter to her; but she had made a change that was too radical to undo now and, besides, she was discovering that trees do not feel things very urgently. She settled back for a long low-key sort of contentment, rustling her leaves about to make the best of the sun's heat on them. It was like a sigh.

After a while, a certain activity among her roots aroused a mild arboreal curiosity in her. With senses that were rapidly atrophying, she perceived a middle-sized iron-gray animal with a sparse bristly coat which was diligently applying its long snout to the task of eating her three-cornered nuts. The animal was decidedly snaggletoothed. It was lean and had a sharp corner to the center of its back, as if that was all that remained of a wiry man's military bearing. It seemed to sense her attention, for it began to rub itself affectionately against her gray trunk—which still showed vestiges of rounded legs within it.

Ah well, thought the tree, and considerately let fall another shower of beech mast for it.

That was long ago. They say that Phega still stands on the hill. She is one of the beech trees that stand on the hill that always holds the last rays of the sun, but so many of the trees in that wood are so old that there is no way to tell which one she is. All the trees show vestiges of limbs in their trunks and all are given at times to inexplicable thrashings in their boughs, as if in memory of the agony of Phega's transformation. In the autumn their leaves turn the color of Phega's hair and often fall only in spring, as though they cling harder than most leaves in honor of the sun.

There is nothing to eat their nuts now. The wild boar vanished from there centuries ago, though the name stayed. The maps usually call the place Boar's Hill.

THE WORST KIDS
IN THE WORLD

BARBARA ROBINSON

The Herdmans, "the worst kids in the world," are out to wreck the church Nativity play. They are unstoppable and as the play begins everyone fears the worst. But as the story of Jesus's birth unfolds everybody is taken by surprise—especially the Herdmans.

O N THE NIGHT of the pageant we didn't have any supper because Mother forgot to fix it. My father said that was all right. Between Mrs. Armstrong's telephone calls and the pageant rehearsals, he didn't expect supper anymore.

"When it's all over," he said, "we'll go someplace and have hamburgers." But Mother said when it was all over she might want to go some place and hide.

"We've never once gone through the whole thing," she said. "I don't know what's going to happen. It may be the first Christmas pageant in history where Joseph and the Wise Men get in a fight, and Mary runs away with the baby."

She might be right, I thought, and I wondered what all of us in the angel choir ought to do in case that happened. It would be dumb for us just to stand there singing about the Holy Infant if Mary had run off with him.

But nothing seemed very different at first.

There was the usual big mess all over the place—baby angels getting poked in the eye by other baby angels' wings and grumpy shepherds stumbling over their bathrobes. The spotlight swooped back and forth and up and down till it made you sick at your stomach to look at it and, as usual, whoever was playing the piano pitched "Away in a Manger" so high we could hardly hear it, let alone sing it. My father says "Away in a Manger" always starts out sounding like a closetful of mice.

But everything settled down, and at 7:30 the pageant began.

While we sang "Away in a Manger," the ushers lit candles all around the church, and the spotlight came on to be the star. So you really had to know the words to "Away in a Manger" because you couldn't see anything—not even Alice Wendleken's Vaseline eyelids.

After that we sang two verses of "O, Little Town of Bethlehem," and then we were supposed to hum some more "O, Little Town of Bethlehem" while Mary and Joseph came in from a side door. Only they didn't come right away. So we hummed and hummed and hummed, which is boring and also very hard, and before long doesn't sound like any song at all—more like an old refrigerator.

"I knew something like this would happen," Alice Wendleken whispered to me. "They didn't come at all! We won't have any Mary and Joseph—and now what are we supposed to do?"

I guess we would have gone on humming till we all turned blue, but we didn't have to. Ralph and Imogene were there all right, only for once they didn't come through the door pushing each other out of the way. They just stood there for a minute as if they weren't sure they were in the right place—because of the candles, I guess, and the church being full of people. They looked like the people you see on the six o'clock news—refugees, sent to wait in some strange ugly place, with all their boxes and sacks around them.

It suddenly occurred to me that this was just the way it must have been for the real Holy Family, stuck away in a barn by people who didn't much care what happened to them. They couldn't have been very neat and tidy either, but more like *this* Mary and Joseph (Imogene's veil was cockeyed as usual, and Ralph's hair stuck out all around his ears). Imogene had the baby doll but she wasn't carrying it the way she was supposed to, cradled in her arms. She had it slung up over her shoulder, and before she put it in the manger she thumped it twice on the back.

I heard Alice gasp and she poked me. "I don't think it's very nice to burp the baby Jesus," she whispered, "as if he had colic." Then she poked me again. "Do you suppose he could have had colic?"

77

I said, "I don't know why not," and I didn't. He *could* have had colic, or been fussy, or hungry like any other baby. After all, that was the whole point of Jesus—that he didn't come down on a cloud like something out of "Amazing Comics," but that he was born and lived . . . a real person.

Right away we had to sing "While Shepherds Watched Their Flocks by Night"—and we had to sing very loud, because there were more shepherds than there were anything else, and they made so much noise, banging their crooks around like a lot of hockey sticks.

Next came Gladys, from behind the angel choir, pushing people out of the way and stepping on everyone's feet. Since Gladys was the only one in the pageant who had anything to say she made the most of it: "Hey! Unto you a child is born!" she hollered, as if it was, for sure, the best news in the world. And all the shepherds trembled, sore afraid—of Gladys, mainly, but it looked good anyway.

Then came three carols about angels. It took that long to get the angels in because they were all primary kids and they got nervous and cried and forgot where they were supposed to go and bent their wings in the door and things like that.

We got a little rest then, while the boys sang "We Three Kings of Orient Are," and everybody in the audience shifted around to watch the Wise Men march up the aisle.

"What have they got?" Alice whispered.

I didn't know, but whatever it was, it was heavy—Leroy almost dropped it. He didn't have his frankincense jar either, and Claude and Ollie didn't have anything although they were supposed to bring the gold and the myrrh.

"I knew this would happen," Alice said for the second time. "I bet it's something awful."

"Like what?"

"Like . . . a burnt offering. You know the Herdmans."

Well, they did burn things, but they hadn't burned this yet. It was a ham—and right away I knew where it came from. My father was on the church charitable works committee—they give away food baskets at Christmas, and this was the Herdman's food-basket ham. It still had the ribbon around it, saying Merry Christmas.

"I'll bet they stole that!" Alice said.

"They did not. It came from their food basket, and if they want to give away their own ham I guess they can do it." But even if the Herdmans didn't like ham (that was Alice's *next* idea) they had never before in their lives given anything away except lumps on the head. So you had to be impressed.

Leroy dropped the ham in front of the manger. It looked funny to see a ham there instead of the fancy bath-salts jars we always used for the myrrh and the frankincense. And then they went and sat down in the only space that was left.

While we sang "What Child Is This?" the Wise Men were supposed to confer among themselves and then leave by a different door, so everyone would understand that they were going home another way. But the Herdmans forgot, or didn't want to, or something, because they didn't confer and they didn't leave either. They just sat there, and there wasn't anything anyone could do about it.

"They're ruining the whole thing!" Alice whispered, but they weren't at all. As a matter of fact, it made perfect sense for the Wise Men to sit down and rest, and I said so.

"They're supposed to have come a long way. You wouldn't expect them just to show up, hand over the ham, and leave!"

As for ruining the whole thing, it seemed to me that the Herdmans had improved the pageant a lot, just by doing what came naturally—like burping the baby, for instance, or thinking a ham would make a better present than a lot of perfumed oil.

Usually, by the time we got to "Silent Night," which was always the last carol, I was fed up with the whole thing and couldn't wait for it to be over. But I didn't feel that way this time. I almost wished for the pageant go on, with the Herdmans in charge, to see what else they would do that was different.

Maybe the Wise Men would tell Mary about their problem with Herod, and she would tell them to go back and lie their heads off. Or Joseph might go with them and get rid of Herod once and for all. Or Joseph and Mary might ask the Wise Men to take the Christ Child with them, figuring that no one would think to look there.

I was so busy planning new ways to save the baby Jesus that I missed the beginning of "Silent Night," but it was all right because everyone sang "Silent Night," including the audience. We sang all the verses too, and when we got to "Son of God, Love's pure light" I happened to look at Imogene and I almost dropped my hymn book on a baby angel.

Everyone had been waiting all this time for the Herdmans to do something absolutely unexpected. And sure enough, that was what happened.

Imogene Herdman was crying.

In the candlelight her face was all shiny with tears and she didn't even bother to wipe them away. She just sat there—awful old Imogene—in her crookedy veil, crying and crying and crying.

Well. It *was* the best Christmas pageant we ever had.

Everybody said so, but nobody seemed to know why. When it was over people stood around the lobby of the church talking about what was different this year. There was something special, everyone said—they couldn't put their finger on what.

Mrs. Wendleken said, "Well, Mary the mother of Jesus had a black eye; that was something special. But only what you might expect," she added.

She meant that it was the most natural thing in the world for a Herdman to have a black eye. But actually nobody hit Imogene and she didn't hit anyone else. Her eye wasn't really black either, just all puffy and swollen. She had walked into the corner of the choir-robe cabinet, in a kind of daze—as if she had just caught on to the idea of God, and the wonder of Christmas.

And this was the funny thing about it all. For years, I'd thought about the wonder of Christmas, and the mystery of Jesus' birth, and never really understood it. But now, because of the Herdmans, it didn't seem so mysterious after all.

When Imogene had asked me what the pageant was about, I told her it was about Jesus, but that was just part of it. It was about a new baby, and his mother and father who were in a lot of trouble—no money, no place to go, no doctor, nobody they knew. And then, arriving from the East (like my uncle from New Jersey) some rich friends.

But Imogene, I guess, didn't see it that way. Christmas just came over her all at once, like a case of chills and fever. And so she was crying, and walking into the furniture.

Afterward there were candy canes and little tiny Testaments for everyone, and a poinsettia plant for my mother from the whole Sunday school. We put the costumes away and folded up the collapsible manger, and just before we left, my father snuffed out the last of the tall white candles.

"I guess that's everything," he said as we stood at the back of the church. "All over now. It was quite a pageant." Then he looked at my mother. "What's that you've got?"

"It's the ham," she said. "They wouldn't take it back. They wouldn't take any candy either, or any of the little Bibles. But Imogene did ask me for a set of the Bible-story pictures, and she took out the Mary picture and said it was exactly right, whatever that means."

I think it meant that no matter how she herself was, Imogene liked the idea of the Mary in the picture—all pink and white and pure-looking, as if she never washed the dishes or cooked supper or did anything at all except have Jesus on Christmas Eve.

But as far as I'm concerned, Mary is always going to look a lot like Imogene Herdman—sort of nervous and bewildered, but ready to clobber anyone who laid a hand on her baby. And the Wise Men are always going to be Leroy and his brothers, bearing ham.

When we came out of the church that night it was cold and clear, with crunchy snow underfoot and bright, bright stars overhead. And I thought about the Angel of the Lord —Gladys, with her skinny legs and her dirty sneakers sticking out from under her robe, yelling at all of us, everywhere:

"Hey! Unto you a child is born!"

THE FAT GIRL'S
VALENTINE

ANN PILLING

from The Big Pink

The pain of being a fat girl is explored in The Big Pink. *Here, on Valentine's Day, the tubby heroine Angela Collis-Browne discovers that she has not, after all, been overlooked.*

CRASH! A TERRIFIC NOISE broke into Angela's dream and woke her up. It was still dark in The Big Pink, and the humps all round her merely stirred gently, and burrowed deeper into their bedding. They were used to Colonel Barrington-Ward firing off his gun at seven every morning.

She lay quite still, glad to have a bit of peace and quiet before the others started moving. The rising bell wouldn't go for another twenty minutes, she could slip off and wash in private, while the rest dozed. She hated the stares she got when she stood at the washbasins in her baggy nightie. Mum had bought her two from Evans Outsize. She knew she was overweight but these were ridiculous. Sophie Sharman had laughed out loud when she saw them. That girl verged on the lunatic, Angela had decided.

There was something different about today, she thought, brushing her teeth, something was happening. But she was still half-asleep and she couldn't think what it was for a minute. Then she remembered, today was Valentine's Day and they were having this funny old-fashioned "dance" in the evening, the dance Auntie Pat wanted chopping . . . But before that, *cards.*

She wouldn't get any and she intended to keep well away from the boarders' pigeonholes. If there was a letter from Mum and Dad it could wait till break. There was always a little group of girls opening their mail and reading bits out: they sometimes got letters from boys. There'd been a lot of speculation last night, after Lights Out, about who might get Valentines, and about Sophie Sharman's "boyfriend," in their village, someone called Francis.

"His name's Stan, actually," Kath had told her at supper. "Stan Arnold. Not exactly romantic, is it?"

No. Not like Sebastian.

"And he's not her boyfriend, he just lives next door." The Broughtons and the Sharmans lived in the same village, so Sophie was a bit silly to claim that she was "going out" with Stan Arnold, and as for pretending his name was Francis . . .

Jane Bragg went down for the post the minute she was dressed. She came back smirking, with four letters. "One for Lorna—"

"It's from Grandma," the girl said, disappointed, looking at the writing. "I hope there's some money in it."

"Two for Soph . . . nothing for me . . . and one for you, Angela."

"Oh, thanks." She held her hand out for the usual blue air-letter and its funny-looking stamp, but Bragg gave her a thick white envelope. They all stared, and waited for her to undo it. "You've got a Valentine," Bragg said. "Aren't you sly, not telling us! Anything from Francis, Soph?"

"No," the Boss said, in a dangerous voice. Rotten old

Stan. At Christmas he'd hinted that he might send one. His ears were gigantic, and he had very thin blonde hair, but at least he was male.

Angela turned her back on the others and sat down on her bed, facing the window. This had got to be a joke. In the first place, she didn't know any boys, apart from the ones at The Comp, and it wouldn't be them. She hadn't got any brothers or cousins who might have done it for a laugh, and there wasn't anybody else.

At first she didn't really look at the envelope properly, she was too busy listening to what might be going on in the dormitory. If it was from Them there'd be a silence.

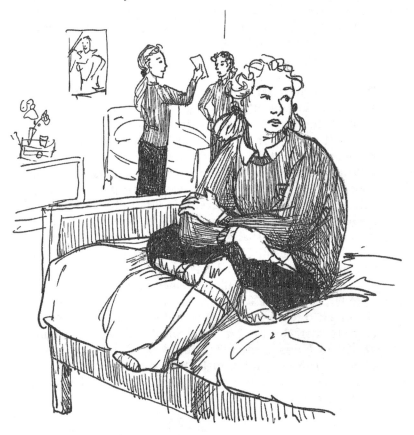

They were too clumsy to cover up their tracks. But The Big Pink was filled with the usual pre-lesson bustle, the scrape and squeak of bed-making, Lorna moaning on about her vanished pajama bottoms, Bragg's radio tuned in to the wail of Radio One.

It had been posted first-class, yesterday afternoon, in High Wycombe. The town was eight miles away, across the neat tidy hills. That meant it was local.

Now for the writing, a flowing italic in bold black ink. She didn't dare get Seb's gardening list out of her locker but she knew that this was the same, she'd seen it on that birthday card, the one for his sister at Oxford.

She wasn't doing anything else with the envelope, not yet. She'd put it in the little red book-bag she carried round school with her, and not look at it again until she was sitting somewhere absolutely private.

It wasn't the most romantic place to open your first Valentine, locked in a lavatory in the junior cloakroom, with all the flushings and noises off, but at least they couldn't get at her in there, not unless they squeezed through the gap at the top of the door.

When she saw the card she knew it was from him. If it had been Sophie's lot it would have been plastered with glittery hearts and flowers. But what she saw was a reproduction of an old painting, all browns and golds, a young woman in a shabby room, looking out of a window at a ship setting sail. She turned it over and read the back. It was called *Longing* and it was from the Victorian Collection, Whitworth Gallery, Manchester.

So far, everything felt right. He knew she came from up North. He'd told her that Mavis in the paper shop was his favorite character in *Coronation Street* and she'd told him she liked Hilda Ogden. This card wouldn't have been chosen by three spiteful girls; they thought love was all slop, and whispering in corners. They'd think a beautiful card like this was dead boring.

86

Inside, in the same black italic, four lines of a poem had been written out neatly:

> *A ship there is, and she sails the sea,*
> *She's loaded deep as deep can be,*
> *But not so deep as the love I'm in,*
> *I know not if I sink or swim.*

Underneath it said "Be my Valentine—please." Then simply "Sebastian."

She looked at the writing again and her heart flipped over. It had to be him, he'd listened to her singing when he was outside, doing the garden. Nobody else knew the words of that song. And how brilliant to have found a card with a ship on.

Of course, it didn't mean that Sebastian actually *loved* her, that would be ridiculous. He was eighteen at least, and going up to Oxford. But it did mean he must quite like her, and she liked him. It was a perfect Valentine: she would always treasure it.

For the rest of the day she thought of little else. She drifted through lessons in a kind of daze, hearing nothing of what was said, seeing nothing, except that Victorian girl staring out of her window at the tall white sails, hearing the music of the song inside her head.

Dr. Crispin told her off for not paying attention, and Mossy shouted at her, when she lost her place in the novel they were reading. Ivy Green stuck her in goal again and once again it rained. But Angela didn't even notice. She let five goals through and got sworn at, but she didn't care; she was much too busy thinking about her envelope and its secret contents. Whenever her mind wandered over to what was hidden in the bottom of her little red bag, she was warmed through by a quiet glow of pure happiness.

If Pat Parkin had her way this was the very last Valentine Dance there was ever going to be. Of all the events left over from the Rimmer days, it was the one she disliked most. She couldn't understand why the girls enjoyed it so much, and why they got so excited about all the dressing up. Next year she was going to organize a disco, Colonel or no Colonel.

She was so unenthusiastic about the whole affair, she didn't bother with fancy dress. When they saw her arrive in a neat gray suit, the whole school was disappointed. "Last year she came as a witch, broomstick and everything. Sensible, wasn't it?" Kath Broughton told Angela.

The Dance was a red-letter day for The Moat because Boys came. In Kings Bretherton there was a small school called St. Antony's and it always got an invitation. The snag was that none of the boys was over thirteen. You danced with one of the junior masters if you were lucky, if unlucky you got landed with a pimply twelve-year-old. As there were rather more juniors than tall handsome masters, most of the girls danced with each other.

They'd all been let loose in the art room at the weekend, to make their costumes. Matron had presided over a mountain of assorted jumble, and she'd helped with cutting out, pinning, and tacking together. People climbed in and out of huge skirts and tried on curious hats, and there was a lot of tittering. Angela rather enjoyed it, in spite of Auntie Pat, who came snooping round periodically to see what they were all doing.

Hettie and Kath won the prize for the best outfit; they went as a duo, dressed as Popeye and Olive Oyl. Kath had great cotton-wool biceps tied to her arms with string and Het carried an outsize tin of spinach. The AA went as a pop group called The Dazzle. They'd used three cans of gold spray paint and covered themselves with Christmas tree glitter. Jane Bragg had hidden her pocket tape recorder down the front of her jeans and they went jazzing around to the noise of the Top Forty.

Sophie was furious when they didn't win. Thank goodness it wasn't me, Angela was thinking, otherwise she'd have said it was "favoritism." She'd gone as a letter-box, with "Post Early for Christmas" painted on the side.

It had been a stroke of genius, making that big cardboard tube for herself. A pillar box was one huge curve so her bulges were safely hidden. The lid came off so she could snatch a bit of air, if it got too stuffy, but for most of the evening she communicated through the slit. Although she was on the large side, Angela had very small feet. Kath and Het had collapsed laughing when they saw a letter-box tripping daintily across the playground (she'd decided to practice, in case walking proved difficult). Angela had laughed too; nothing could touch her today, she'd got Seb's Valentine card at the bottom of her red bag. It was the happiest she'd been since she'd come to The Moat.

Mossy arrived dressed as a Sea-Green Maiden in a fabulous 1920s evening dress covered with sequins. She'd sprayed green stuff on her hair, and she was wearing bright green makeup. Angela was impressed. Most of the staff had taken the evening off, and those who'd come hadn't made much of an effort. Dr. Crispin was at large though, dressed as a miserable-looking clown, and Miss Bunting came as The Little Match Girl, with her sharp bird-like face looking out of the rags and tatters.

Nobody was bothering with Mossy. Since that embarrassing outburst in English she'd made Sophie's class read novels, or do grammar exercises. It was as if she'd given up trying with Form 3, and it was The Boss's fault. Angela detested her now. Good clean *hate*. There was no other word for it.

"Will you dance with me, Miss Moss?" she said, raising her lid. It had taken some doing, but she'd been determined to ask. She felt really sorry for Mossy.

"Is it Angela? You look rather different in that, dear. Of course I will. Delighted . . ." and they were off, trundling slowly round the floor to a scratchy record of "Come Dancing," an aged mermaid in a clinch with a tubby letter-box.

"I like your costume, Miss Moss, you look great," it said, and they rolled past The Dazzle. Sophie Sharman heard, and pursed her lips in smug disapproval. "Sucking up," she whispered to Jane Bragg. "Typical, isn't it? And look at Mossy. How pathetic to wear a thing like that at her age."

Bragg rather admired the senior English teacher for making such a big effort, especially after the way Form 3 had treated her, and she secretly thought that the 1920s dress was a knockout. But Sophie was in a foul mood because they'd not won first prize, so she decided to keep her mouth shut.

"It's a pity there are so few of the male species, don't you think?" Mossy said, as they lumbered about. (Angela's arms stuck out of the tube at right angles, so getting a firm grip on her sea-green partner took some doing.) "You know what they say, dear, 'The zest goes out of a beautiful waltz. When you're dancing it bust to bust . . .'"

"I beg your pardon," said the letter-box politely, "I didn't quite catch that?"

"I said it's a pity there aren't more *men*, dear!"

Everyone turned round and stared at them. People had been tittering quietly since Mossy and the letter-box had taken the floor; now they laughed out loud. "I'm a man," a voice said cheerfully. "Can I steal your partner for a bit, Miss Moss? It's not often I get the chance to chat up a letter-box."

"Well of course, dear, don't let me stand in your way." And the Sea-Green Maiden swished her long beads at him and wafted away toward the food. "I'll go and see what Gladys has dreamed up," she said. "That little match girl looks as if she needs stoking up a bit, don't you think? Can't have her dying on me, before *Butterflies*."

Angela peeped out through her slit. She knew the voice, though Seb was hardly recognizable in his fancy dress; he'd come as a punk rocker, skin-tight, shiny pink pants, pink T-shirt, black jacket, one enormous black earring and his hair combed up in stiff blue peaks. "Shall we dance?" he said.

91

Angela hesitated. "I—I can't very well, it's the tube; my arms are at a funny angle. I'll have to take this off for a minute. I'm terribly hot. Do you mind holding it," and she gave him her lid.

"Oh, it's *you*, Angela."

"Yes." Her voice was quite faint, she *felt* faint. His card had been enough for one day, she wasn't sure that she could actually hold a conversation with him, it was too embarrassing.

"Come on, let's have a whirl." Angela stuck her arms out obligingly and Sebastian grabbed them. He moved fast but she could only take little steps. She felt like a Dalek inside that tube.

"Anne looks fabulous, doesn't she?" she whispered. "The Sixth Form hadn't got time to make anything, they were doing an exam or something, so they were allowed to use their old play costumes."

Anne Arnott and Ginnie Griffiths had come as Toad and Ratty. Even with her face powdered green and wearing a check cap and motoring goggles, the Head Girl had style.

"How's Muffet doing?" she asked Sebastian as the record clicked off and they ground to a clumsy halt in the middle of the floor. "I couldn't come at the weekend. I spent most of the time making this." She tried to adjust her tube, it was too hot inside all that cardboard. If she'd known he was coming she wouldn't have dressed as a letter-box, she'd have gone for something rather more flattering.

"Oh, he's great, he's in love with my mother. Don't worry about him."

"I'm not worrying," she said, and she sounded rather solemn. She'd taken her lid off again now, shaken her hair out and was staring steadily into his eyes.

Seb stared back, slightly unnerved. Angela Collis-Browne had a very direct gaze. What a funny girl.

"Thanks very much for the card, Seb." As she said it her insides knotted themselves together, and a great lump came into her throat.

"What card?" He sounded genuinely puzzled and yet he was smiling, smiling all the time.

"The one you sent me in the post, with the girl and the ship on . . . you *know. Longing.*"

"Oh, that," he said blankly, but she was watching him very carefully. There had been a definite pause, just a second too long, and his eyes had gone all over the place.

Angela knew, beyond all possible doubt, that someone else had sent that Valentine.

She crept away, quite gracefully for a letter-box, and with painful slowness got herself up the stairs, along the corridor, and into The Big Pink. She shut the door, then struggled out of the tube, wrecking it in the process. Mossy had wanted to preserve the letter-box for her Christmas Pageant, but Angela spent a good five minutes trampling it flat, before kicking it savagely under a bed.

"Temper, temper'" said a sour, familiar voice. The lead singer of The Dazzle was standing in the doorway. "What on earth's the matter with you?" she added, when she got no response.

"I don't feel well," Angela said in a strangled voice. "That red paint had an awful smell and I was too hot inside that thing."

"Well, if you will insist on—"

"Oh leave me *alone*, Sophie Sharman. I'm going to bed."

She took everything off, there, under the harsh main light, in full view of The Boss (she usually took refuge in a helpful tent arrangement Mum had made, out of terry toweling). She left everything in a heap on the floor, plopped her rosebud nightie over her head, and clambered aboard, uncombed, unwashed. Then she pulled the covers right up to her ears so the world was blotted out. The others came in, in ones and twos, and started getting undressed and talking about the Dance . . . about *her*, no doubt.

Angela didn't bother to listen. She was too busy crying.

A RAILWAY STORY

GUY DE MAUPASSANT

I

THE COMPARTMENT HAD BEEN full all the way from Cannes. The passengers chatted among themselves, for they were all acquainted. When they reached Tarascon, someone said: "This is where all those murders were committed." And they started talking about the mysterious assassin who for two years now had been occasionally treating himself to the life of the odd traveler. Everyone had a theory and everyone said what he thought: the women shivered as they stared into the black night on the other side of the windows, afraid they might see a man's head suddenly framed in the glass of the door. And they all began telling frightening stories about ill-fated encounters, about people traveling aboard express trains who had found themselves alone in a compartment with a madman, or had sat for hours opposite a suspicious character.

Every man there knew a story in which he played a major role, for they had all browbeaten, floored, or throttled some evildoer in amazing circumstances and always with admirable daring and presence of mind. A doctor, who spent each winter on the south coast, also offered to recount an adventure:

Now I, he said, have never had the opportunity of testing my courage in the kind of tight corners you've been talking about. But I did know a woman, one of my patients, now dead, who had the oddest thing happen to her which was most mysterious and very, very sad.

She was Russian, the Countess Marie Baranow, a lady of the highest rank and an exquisite beauty. You know how beautiful Russian women can be, or at least the way they seem beautiful to our way of thinking: dainty nose, delicate mouth, close-set eyes of an indefinable color, a sort of bluey-gray, and that cool grace which seems a mite unfeeling! There is something cruel and attractive about them, and they are both distant and yielding, loving and aloof, a mixture which no Frenchman could ever resist. Still, perhaps it's just differences of race and type which make me see all these things in them.

For a number of years, her doctor had been of the opinion that her lungs were seriously affected, and he kept trying to persuade her to go off to the south of France. But she stubbornly refused to leave Saint Petersburg. Anyhow, last autumn, believing that there was little hope left for her, the doctor informed her husband who immediately ordered his wife to leave for Menton.

She boarded the train and traveled alone in her carriage, her retinue occupying a separate compartment. She sat rather dejectedly near the door, watching the fields and villages speed by and feeling very alone and utterly forsaken, for she had no children, very few relations, and a husband who did not love her anymore and had sent her off to the other side of the world instead of coming with her, just as a sick servant is packed off to hospital.

Each time they stopped at a station, her servant Ivan

came along to ask if his mistress needed anything. He was very much the old retainer, blindly obedient and always ready to carry out whatever orders she gave him.

Night fell. The train was traveling at full speed. She was too restless to sleep. Then she thought she would count the money, in French gold coins, which her husband had given her just before she left. She opened her small money-bag and poured a gleaming river of metal onto her knees.

Suddenly a breath of cold air struck her face. She looked up in surprise. The carriage door had opened. Alarmed, Countess Marie quickly threw a shawl over the money in her lap and waited. Moments went by, then a man appeared. He was bareheaded, nursed an injured hand, and was breathing hard. He wore evening dress. Closing the door behind him, he looked at her with eyes that gleamed, then wrapped a handkerchief around his wrist which was bleeding badly.

The young woman felt faint with fear. It was obvious that this man had seen her counting her money and had come to rob and kill her.

He continued to stare at her, still gasping for breath, his face twitching, and clearly ready to leap upon her. All at once he said: "Please! Don't be afraid!"

She did not reply, for she could not open her mouth and was aware that her heart was pounding and her ears buzzing.

He continued: "I won't harm you."

Still she did not speak, but a sudden movement which she made brought her knees together and her gold streamed onto the carpet like rainwater pouring off a gutter. The man stared in surprise at the river of metal then bent down to pick it up.

She stood up in a panic and, letting the rest of her money fall to the floor, rushed to the door intending to throw herself out onto the track. But he anticipated what she was about to do, made a dash for her, grabbed her in his arms, and, holding her by the wrists, forced her to sit down: "Listen. I won't harm you, and to prove it I'll pick up your money and give it all back to you. But unless you help me get across the frontier, it's all up with me, I'm as good as dead. I can't tell you any more. In an hour, we'll be at the last station in Russia; an hour and twenty minutes from now, we'll just be crossing the imperial border. If you do not help me, I am done for. But I haven't killed anyone, stolen anything, or done anything dishonorable. This I swear. I can't tell you any more than that."

Getting down on his knees, he picked up all the gold, even looking under the seats and scouring the corners where coins might have rolled. Then, when her little leather bag was full again, he held it out to her without another word and went and sat down on the other side of the compartment.

After this, neither of them stirred. She sat motionless and silent, still weak with terror but slowly regaining her composure. For his part, the man did not move a finger but remained completely immobile, sitting bolt upright, with his eyes staring straight ahead and looking as pale as a corpse. From time to time she glanced quickly at him and then away. He was about 30, very handsome, and all the indications were that he was a gentleman.

The train steamed on into the darkness, piercing the night with its shrill whistles, slowing down at times and then picking up again. But suddenly it dropped its speed, whistled three times, and came to a halt.

Ivan appeared at the door to ask for orders.

Countess Marie glanced one last time at her strange companion and then, in a voice that shook, spoke sharply to her servant: "Ivan, you are to go back to the Count. I shan't be needing you anymore."

Ivan opened his eyes wide in bewilderment. He stammered: "But . . . mistress . . ."

She went on: "You won't be coming with me. I've changed my mind. I want you to remain in Russia. Here, take this money. There's enough to get you home. Give me your hat and coat."

The old man, greatly puzzled, removed his hat and handed over his coat, obeying without question, for he was used to the sudden fancies and irresistible whims of his betters. Then he went away with tears in his eyes.

The train set off again, heading now for the frontier.

Then the Countess said to the man: "These things are for you. You are Ivan, my servant. I set just one condition on what I am about to do: you will never speak to me, not one word, not to thank me or for any other purpose."

The stranger gave a slight bow but said not a word.

Soon they stopped again and uniformed officials inspected the train. The Countess showed them her papers and motioning toward the man seated on the far side of the compartment, said: "That is my servant, Ivan. Here's his passport."

The train set off once more. The two of them remained alone together all through the night without speaking.

The next morning the train stopped at a German station and the stranger got out. But at the door he paused and said: "Forgive me if I break my promise. But I have deprived you of your servant and it would be only right if I should take his place. Is there anything that you need?"

She answered him coolly: "Go and tell my maid I want her."

He went. He then disappeared.

But thereafter, whenever she left the train and went into station refreshment rooms, she kept noticing him in the distance, watching her. They finally reached Menton.

II

The doctor paused for a few moments and then went on:

One day, I was seeing patients in my surgery when a tall young man came in and said: "Doctor, I've come to see you because I would like to know how Countess Marie Baranow is. She does not know me, but I am a friend of her husband."

"There is no hope," I replied. "She will never return to Russia."

The man suddenly started sobbing, then left, staggering like a drunken man.

The same evening, I informed the Countess that a stranger had come to see me asking about her health. She seemed troubled and told me the story which I have just told you. And she added: "This man, whom I do not know, follows me everywhere like my shadow. I see him every time I go out. He looks at me in the oddest way, but he's never said a word to me." She thought for a moment before continuing: "I'll wager he's there outside my house now."

She rose from her *chaise longue*, went over and drew the curtains, and pointed out the man who had called on me who was indeed there, sitting on a bench on the promenade looking up at the house. He saw us, got up, and walked away without turning around once.

From then on, I became an observer of an amazing and distressing phenomenon—the unspoken love of these two people who knew virtually nothing about each other.

He loved her with the devotion of a rescued animal which is grateful and loyal until death. Each day he would come and ask: "How is she?", for he realized I had guessed the truth. And when he saw her pass by looking weaker and paler each day, he wept in the most dreadful fashion.

And she would say: "I only ever spoke to him once. Yet I feel I have known that strange man for twenty years."

And when they happened to meet, she always returned his bow with a grave but charming smile. I sensed that she was happy. I felt that she, who was so alone and fully aware that she was dying, was truly happy to be loved in this way, repectfully, steadfastly, exaltedly, poetically, with a devotion which knew no limits. Yet she remained faithful to her extravagant obsession and despairingly went on refusing to meet him or ask his name or speak to him. She said: "No, no, it would destroy the rare bond between us. We must remain strangers to each other."

On his side he, too, had a quixotic streak in his character, for he did nothing to get close to her. He was determined to keep to the end the absurd promise never to speak to her which he had made in the railway carriage.

During her long periods of exhaustion, she would often rise from her *chaise longue* and pull back her curtain just a little to see if he was there, outside, beneath her windows.

And when she had seen him, sitting motionless on his usual bench, she would lie down again with a smile on her lips.

She died one morning, at about ten o'clock. As I was leaving the house he came up to me, his face grief-stricken. He had heard the news already.

"I would like to see her, just for a moment, in your presence," he said.

I took him by the arm and went back into the house.

When he was standing by the dead woman's bedside, he grasped her hand and kissed it interminably. Then he fled like a mad thing.

The doctor paused once more.

"That," he went on, "is the strangest tale about railways I know. Still, you've got to admit that folk can be very peculiar indeed."

A woman said quietly: "Those two weren't half as mad as you make out . . . They were . . . They were . . ." But she couldn't go on, because she had started to cry. And since everyone immediately began talking about other things to take her mind off it, we never did find out what she meant.

ORPHEUS AND EURYDICE

JAMES REEVES

A Greek myth

APOLLO, GOD OF THE SUN and greatest of all musicians, had a son by the Muse Calliope. The Muses were nine goddesses who lived on Mount Helicon and inspired poets, writers, and musicians. The son of Apollo and Calliope was called Orpheus.

As might be expected of the son of such gifted parents, Orpheus proved to have more than ordinary talent for music. His father gave him a lyre of great beauty, cunningly fashioned so that the music of its seven strings was of unusual power and sweetness. But greater than the sweetness of the lyre was the skill of its owner. As the young man, dark-haired and with shining eyes, went about the countryside singing to the strains of his lyre, not only did men and women marvel to hear him; even mountains seemed to be raising their heads in wonder. The streams stayed their rushing to listen to him, and even the very rocks lost some of their hardness at the sound of his music. He became familiar among the woods and mountains of Thrace, which were inhabited by wild animals. But Orpheus went in no fear of even the fiercest creature; for such was the power of his music that the very wolves and lions would lie down at his feet and draw in their claws, lulled to gentleness as the young man's fingers moved over the strings of his lyre. The harmless creatures, the fawn and the antelope, would stretch themselves out beside the lion, sensing that even the king of beasts would not harm them so long as Orpheus played and sang. The trees crowded together about the musician, giving shade to him and his audience; the winds were still, and in the branches sat the dove and the eagle, side by side. Never before had such music charmed the ear of man and beast alike.

In Thrace lived the nymphs of stream and woodland, and they too came to listen to Orpheus. The wood nymphs were called Dryads, and among them the most beautiful was Eurydice. No sooner did she cast eyes on the young musician than she fell in love with him. Raising his head from the lyre, Orpheus as quickly fell in love with the Dryad, and resolved to marry her. Their courting was not long, and soon they had agreed to become man and wife. But at the wedding ceremony Fate was not on their side. For when Hymen, the god of marriage, held aloft the lighted torch, it burned, not with a clear, golden flame, but with black smoke which drifted over the assembly in a thick and ominous cloud. So the eyes of the crowd, instead of being filled with joy, smarted with tears of pain. In vain did Orpheus play his best; in vain the nymphs prayed to the gods to send better omens.

Not long afterward Eurydice and the other Dryads were wandering through the woods when a young man named Aristaeus caught sight of her and determined to win her for himself. He tried to seize her, but she fled from him through the trees, and he pursued her. In her flight Eurydice chanced to step on a snake in the grass. It bit her foot, and she died of the poison. Aristaeus, her pursuer, was a shepherd and a beekeeper, and after the death of Eurydice the nymphs, her companions, poisoned his bees in revenge, so that they died.

So great was the shock to Orpheus that he could not believe Eurydice was really dead. Might not his music, that had moved even stones, soften the hearts of the gods? For they were all-powerful and could give him back his wife if they wished. So Orpheus played upon his lyre more ravishingly than ever, raising his voice in sorrowful lamentation. The gods of the earth were moved, but they could do nothing for him, since the dead do not stay upon the earth but descend into the realm of the stern god Hades and his queen, Persephone. Here in the timeless shades the spirits of the dead wander aimlessly, and never look again upon the green fields and woods of the upper world.

In despair Orpheus went to seek his lost wife in the regions of the dead. He went down into the underworld by a steep and narrow way which began in a gloomy cave. Down and down the path wound until it reached the gray and dreary realm of Hades. Passing through crowds of ghosts, Orpheus made his way toward the throne of the king and queen. At the sight of the wild-eyed musician with his lyre, the god Hades raised his hand for silence and bade the stranger play. With his right hand Orpheus struck the lyre and, lifting his voice, began to plead and mourn in tones which moved the hardest hearts and brought tears to the eyes of many.

"O god and goddess," sang Orpheus, "to whom we must all come at last, listen, I pray, to my tale, for I speak the truth. Perhaps you ask why I, a living man, have come of my own free will to your kingdom. I am not here to spy out the secrets of Hades nor to fight against the monster who guards your gates. I am come to plead for your mercy and to beg you to give back life to my beloved Eurydice, who was slain by the cruel viper when our wedding rites were scarcely over. Give her back to me, I beg, for she has done no harm and broken no vow. Gods of the underworld, we shall all come under your rule in time. When our time has come, we shall give thanks to the gods for our love and our lives, but until she has lived her proper span, give her back to me, I implore you."

So piteously did Orpheus lament, with such skill did he draw harmony from the strings that the inhabitants of Hades came from near and far to hear his music. The ghosts came in crowds, like flocks of birds coming home to roost at dusk, or like showers of dead leaves driven by the autumn wind. There were boys and men, unmarried girls, the spirits of great heroes and of nameless ones who had died in battle on land or sea. All who heard were touched to the heart by the music of Orpheus; all pitied the young man whose loss had inspired him to songs never heard before on earth or in the underworld.

Among those who heard Orpheus were the prisoners in Hades, doomed to suffer eternal punishment for their crimes on earth. Tantalus was one. He was condemned to lie beneath a tree at the edge of a pool. Every time he stretched out his hand to gather fruit, a wind blew the branches out of reach. Every time he approached the pool to quench his thirst, the water drew back. Another was Ixion, whose punishment was to be tied to a wheel which turned forever. When Orpheus sang, the wheel stood still, and Ixion was for a while relieved of his torment. Sisyphus, for his crimes on earth, was condemned to roll a heavy stone up a hill; as soon as it reached the top, it rolled down again, so that his labor was eternal. For the first time he was allowed to rest upon his stone halfway up the hill, while Orpheus lamented. For the first time, too, the cheeks of the Furies were wet with tears. These were among the most terrible deities in Hades—three winged women whose purpose was to avenge crimes against family ties, such as the killing of a parent or child. Some say that their look was made fiercer by writhing serpents which crowned their heads, like the serpents of the gorgon Medusa. Now even the snakes ceased their writhing and hissing to listen to Orpheus.

By the time the song was finished, Persephone, queen of the underworld, could not restrain her pity, and with tear-filled eyes she looked at her husband and pleaded for the life of Eurydice. Hades, stern king, consented, and the young bride was summoned from among the newly arrived ghosts. Limping upon her wounded foot, Eurydice appeared, pale and beautiful, before the throne. Long and lovingly Orpheus looked at her, but he dared not approach until the king had given his judgment. Because of his steadfastness in love, said the king, Orpheus would be allowed to take her back to the earth on one condition: he was to lead the way, and Eurydice would follow. He must not look back at her, even for an instant, until they reached the upper air. If he did, he would lose her once more—this time forever.

Eagerly Orpheus embraced his wife. Then, taking leave of the king and queen, they began the journey back to earth. Orpheus went in front, Eurydice behind, as they had been bidden. Once the gloomy regions of ghosts were passed, they came to a place of terrible darkness and silence, groping their way between rocks and through dark passages where icy water dripped about them, and jagged rocks tore their clothes. Then they began to climb, up and up along the winding track by which Orpheus had come. Panting, he reached a sort of ledge or platform not far from where the track led into the cave where it would end in the light of day. Suddenly a madness overcame Orpheus. A terrible fear for his loved Eurydice made him forget his promise to the king of the underworld. He looked back to see if he could make out her form in the darkness behind him, and in that instant she was lost to him.

A great roll of thunder came from the underworld beneath, as if the Furies were expressing their wrath at Orpheus's forgetfulness. There is no forgiveness in Hades. Amid the thunder Orpheus heard the voice of Eurydice:

"O Orpheus, the Fates are calling me back. Unseen hands are dragging me down. I feel faint, and I no longer have any power to resist."

In vain did Orpheus stretch out his arms to embrace her. She floated like a cloud of gray smoke back into the depths of Hades. He had lost her forever.

For seven months Orpheus wandered amid the desolate rocks and mountains of Thrace, lamenting the second death of Eurydice in strains which softened the stones about him and melted the hard hearts of wolves and lions. But his song had no power to pierce the ears of the guardians of the underworld, and he called down bitter curses upon their heads.

"O gloomy powers," he sang, "O savage Furies, let an everlasting curse fall upon your flinty hearts. Wolves are not too cruel to be moved; granite cliffs are softened by my grief. You alone remain immovable in your unjust and hellish fury against one whose only fault was to love too much the wife you have taken from him."

The story of Orpheus's death is as sad as that of Eurydice's, and more terrible. The Thracian nymphs, Eurydice's former companions, tried to console Orpheus, but he would not listen to them. He wished only to be left to mourn for his wife alone. But they pursued him with sweet songs and wooed him with garlands of flowers.

"Eurydice is dead," they said. "She will never return again. Take another wife. Take one of us, and she will make you happier than ever you were before."

Still Orpheus would not listen, and in the end the nymphs' love was turned to hate. They now wished only to destroy Orpheus.

One day they were celebrating the festival of the god Dionysus. The music and dancing maddened them, and one of them, seeing Orpheus a long way off, cried:

"See, there is the man who scorns us, the man who despises our kindness and love. He no longer deserves to live!"

Swiftly she ran, spear in hand, to where Orpheus was playing a sad lament on his lyre. When she was within range, she hurled the spear. But the spear was turned away from Orpheus by the power of his music. So also were the stones which other maidens threw at the young man.

At this the enraged nymphs lifted their voices in a scream of anger, which utterly drowned the notes of the lyre. Orpheus's music had no longer any power to protect him, and in a moment a spear struck him in the breast and he was killed. Then the shrieking nymphs tore his body limb from limb and flung the remains far and wide. They cut off his head, and threw it, together with the lyre, into the River Hebrus. Such was the revenge of Eurydice's former companions on her unhappy husband. Such was his reward for loving her too dearly.

The head of Orpheus floated slowly down the river, the lyre beside it. His eyes were closed and his black hair, stained with blood, streamed behind him. From his open mouth came a long last lament; and magical notes sounded from the floating lyre, so that the trees along the riverbank bowed their heads in sympathy, and the shores echoed with the dead man's sorrow. At last the head of Orpheus reached the island of Lesbos, where it was buried. The lyre was taken up by the gods and given a place among the stars in heaven. Orpheus's mother, Calliope, and her sister Muses gathered up the torn limbs and buried them in a grove in Libethra. Here, it is said, nightingales sing over the grave of Orpheus with a more piercing sweetness than in any other part of Greece.

The spirit of Orpheus went down to the underworld, where once the living man had been. Eagerly he sought the spirit of his dead Eurydice and together they wander through the gray wastes of Hades, happy in each other's company, happy in the knowledge that never again can they be divided.

BILLIE

ANN PILLING

DAD SAID, "Oh, and he's called Billie by the way," very casually, just like that, as if your name was the last thing that mattered. Robert knew that his father wasn't feeling casual, just the opposite in fact. He was as tense as a drum skin; so was Mum. "Billie," Robert repeated softly, "the three Billy Goats gruff," and he laughed.

His parents flicked uneasy looks at each other, then his mother inspected her hands, waiting for his father to speak. She had wanted to foster a child for so long but Dad hadn't been quite sure and the family discussions had been endless. Now "Billie" was coming and the tension in the house was thickening by the minute.

Robert's little joke obviously hadn't helped. "Now *listen*," his father flashed, "we don't want any funny business about this boy."

"Sorry."

"I should think so," and he bent down to remove a bit of fluff from the carpet.

Mum gave Robert an anxious smile. She knew he was

nervous about the foster child. He'd said he didn't mind at all if they looked after someone for a bit, it might even be good fun, but why for heaven's sake had they made such elaborate preparations? It wasn't just the spare room that had been redecorated, it was a proper "little boy's" room now with Superman wallpaper, but they'd done the bathroom and the kitchen, this room, too, with its expensive new carpet. Billie surely wasn't likely to stay very long.

Liz, his older sister, who was away at music college, wasn't so sure. She'd left home, he was nearly fourteen, and the third child their parents had wanted had never happened. Then this "Billie" had come up for fostering and the Harbournes had been deemed "suitable." They'd hoped—Robert had too—that he might be older, someone who could become a friend. But he was only eight and according to Dad was bringing a few problems with him. They'd been prepared to tell Robert the whole story but he'd said no, not yet. From the bits Liz had let out it all sounded too heartbreaking and he didn't think he could bear it. Let the child come first, and settle in.

The minute he saw him Robert knew Billie spelled trouble. Everything about him felt alien and there was a kind of deep hostility pulsing through him in great waves. Physically he couldn't be more different from the two Harbourne children who were long and gangling with light blond hair and blue eyes; Billie was four-square and thick-set, very swarthy with a mass of tight black curls, his enormous dark eyes two great glossy pools. He had the sort of film-star good looks that turned heads in the street. Next to him the Harbourne children looked wishy-washy, almost two-dimensional.

His first act was to ruin the new living room carpet. At tea, the day he came, Mum, unusually bright and breezy and obviously trying hard to hide her nerves, dropped a bag of sugar which split, scattering its contents all over the kitchen tiles. "Sugar's the very worst thing, Billie" she said, down on her hands and knees with a dustpan and brush. "It gets everywhere, like sand at the seaside, you know." From behind a chair (he always tried to put some solid object between himself and other people, Robert had noticed) the boy watched carefully as she swept up the gray, gritty grains. "Wine's the worst," he said belligerently, "my mam said."

Mrs. Harbourne didn't react, but Robert saw her looking at his father. According to Liz one of Billie's "problems" had been parents who drank, not just one parent, but *both*. So what on earth must have happened to him when they were both drunk at the same time? What else must have gone on in his eight years of life and why, when there was no furniture to hide behind, did his hands always fly up to his face?

In the living room that first night Billie stayed awake for hours, curled up on Mum's knee like a cat, watching television through his fingers. The Harbourne parents had always had strict rules about going to bed, they liked order, routine, cleanliness. But every time Dad tried to prise Billie from Mum's arms he went rigid, doubled himself up on her lap, and let out a spine-chilling, high-pitched squealing noise, like tomcats having a fight. In the end Mr. Harbourne gave up and carried on with his Saturday night ritual, bringing in the usual tray with its two glasses and its half bottle of red wine. They always had a drink at the weekend though Robert was a bit surprised when the wine appeared, in view of what he knew about Billie's parents. The boy asked for a drink too so Dad went back to the kitchen and returned with mugs of hot chocolate. "Here you are, you two," he said. "Put your own sugar in. Let's all drink to Billie," and he gave a rather unconvincing smile.

It seemed to be the signal for Billie to spring out of Mum's lap, very suddenly and silently, like a coiled spring released, to grab the sugar bowl and to scatter its contents over the new carpet, then to water it in with the bottle of

wine. *"Billie!"* cried Mrs. Harbourne. "What on earth are you—" But Dad raised the flat of his hand." It's OK, it's *OK*. No damage done," he said in a whisper as the dark red seeped into the thick pile of the immaculate beige carpet. From behind the television the child peeped out, his fingers laced across his eyes, which were now fixed greedily, with a kind of joy, upon the spreading stain. The mess he'd made seemed to have calmed him down and he went off to bed without a word.

While Dad was upstairs with him Robert helped his mother to attack the carpet. She put salt on it, then soapy water, but the harder she rubbed the worse the great dark patch seemed to become. She was crying as she bent over it, but whether it was for the carpet or for Billie, Robert couldn't quite decide. Every night he threw a tantrum at bedtime, spent hours kicking at his wall, then wandered around the house when they were all asleep, banging doors to wake everybody up. Mornings were even worse because they meant going to school and he hated that. Every day at breakfast, for nearly a week, he waited until Mum's back was turned then spat into Robert's bowl of cornflakes. "Don't react," Dad begged, when he heard about it. Robert didn't. He simply threw the cornflakes away, made himself toast, and ate it walking around the room. But something made him persist with his cornflakes routine. He was a Harbourne and he liked his usual breakfast.

On the Friday Billie ruined the cornflakes for the last time. Gathering together all the spit that he could muster Robert bent over his bowl and gave him the same treatment. The child's mouth dropped open, he slid off his stool, gave Robert a little kick, and waited. "Don't *do* that, Billie, and don't keep spitting into my breakfast. If you kick me again I'll kick you back, *hard*."

There was a long silence in which they stared at one another, Robert's pale blue eyes searching the deep brown pools of Billie's. "OK," he said at last, and he squatted down on the floor and started playing with some toy cars. When it was time for school he went off with Robert quite happily, actually holding his hand as they walked down the street.

"I think you're winning," Mum said, when she heard about it. "He really likes you."

But Robert was still cautious. He'd seen the joy in Billie's face as the wine had spread over the new carpet and he borrowed Dad's tools, bought a padlock, and fitted it onto his bedroom door. After a whole year of saving his paper-round money he'd recently bought himself a hi-fi system. He could just see Billie creeping in, twisting off the delicate pickup arm, gouging great scratch marks across all his records, pulling the tapes from the cassettes. Every day now, before going to school, he carefully locked up his room. He was frightened of the wild, hard energy in Billie, of that awful anger deep inside the small tense body which suddenly broke out for no apparent reason and sent him screeching around the house, flinging himself against the furniture and pulling endlessly at Mum and Dad so he could get up onto their laps, or into their arms.

"He's just a little attention seeker," Robert said one night when Billie, having worn himself out by screaming, had collapsed in bed and actually fallen asleep. This "experiment" of his parents' was beginning to get on his nerves. There was no peace anymore, no order, no family time.

Mum said sadly, "I know, but he's had no love, Robert. All he's ever known is violence and unhappiness. That's all we're trying to do, trying to give him a bit of love. But it's obviously going to take time. Oh, I *do* wish you'd not put that lock on your bedroom door . . ." Regularly, like a record stuck in a groove, she returned to the subject of the padlock. Dad always supported her.

Only when Liz came home for a weekend did they see Robert's side of it. She was studying the violin and on the Saturday night Mrs. Cousins, her old piano teacher, came around so that they could play together. At first Billie sat on Mum's knee and listened. Robert watched him very carefully, thinking the sad, sweet music might calm him down. Dad had explained once that there was a thing

117

called "music therapy," which sometimes helped people to relax and to sort out all their tangled hurt feelings. But Billie was obviously bored. Liz and Mr. Cousins had only played a few bars when he asked to have the television on. When Mum whispered "no" he slid off her lap and crawled under the table where he started banging at the legs with one of his toy trucks.

Mrs. Cousins was very interested in Liz's new bow, an eighteenth birthday present from Grandpa Harbourne, who had once played the violin himself in an important orchestra. "It's a *very* good one, Elizabeth," she said, examining it carefully. "I shouldn't think there was much change out of a thousand pounds, was there?" Liz shrugged. "I don't really know. Grandpa gave it to me. It does play beautifully, doesn't it?"

"I'd no idea a violin bow could be worth so much," Mum said, as they went to the front door with Mrs. Cousins. "We must get it insured. John, you'll have to ring your father."

While everyone was in the hall saying good-bye there was a snapping sound in the living room. Billie, standing on the new carpet, just in front of his wine stain, had broken the bow into two pieces and was waving it slowly round his head, wide-eyed and at peace now, a satisfied little smile on his face. Liz gave a little scream then burst into tears.

For once, Dad wasn't gentle. Without a word he grabbed Billie, took him up to his room and shut the door on them both. It was nearly midnight before he came down again and Billie was still screaming, and kicking at the wall. Nobody got any sleep that night. At breakfast next day everyone was pink-eyed and irritable. Only Billie had slept, blissful in his new Superman bedroom.

They talked for hours that Sunday about whether Billie ought to go back. Liz was still smarting about her ruined bow and rather in favor of getting rid of him. She

brought his cheap cardboard suitcase down from the loft
and dumped it in the hall. Robert said nothing. It seemed
to him that Billie always wrecked the things that people
particularly cared about, the things that gave them joy,
Mum's carpet, for example, the new rose bushes that Dad
had just planted out in the front, which Billie had torn up
and trampled on, Liz's precious bow. It must be that he
himself had never been allowed to love anything, or at
least not love it for very long. Liz had whispered that his
mother used to shut him in a cupboard if he misbehaved
and that she never played with him or allowed him to
have any toys. So he was jealous of the things that other
people had which took them into their own private world,
away from his incessant demands; he had to put an
end to them.

Billie stayed.

Sometimes, late at night, when his parents were
dropping with tiredness and Billie was still kicking at his
bedroom wall, Robert would creep in and read to him. He

liked stories and he would snuggle under the duvet, stick his thumb in his mouth and listen. When at last his eyes started to close Robert would stroke at his cheek and at his thick dark hair. Always, in response, Billie would make gentle purring noises like a satisfied cat. All the anger and rage packed up tightly inside his squat little frame was like a great black tangle of endless string. If only someone could find the end, tease it out gently, and give him release. Dad had hoped the clue to him might be music, but the bow episode had knocked that theory on the head.

Robert decided that Billie needed a pet. He was always mesmerized by animal programs on television and he seemed to understand animals better than people. He even purred or grunted when he was happy, and scratched and spat and bit when something upset him. A pet would be something he could relate to when human beings got too complicated and demanding, something he could give all his love to. For Robert had decided that there *was* a kind of love in Billie.

On the way to school they often passed Boris the chip-shop cat, sitting on its favorite bit of wall. Billie always stopped and fussed the old ginger tom, tickled its flea-bitten ears and kneaded its neck, drawing great rapturous purrings from it. And after the bit of fuss he positively skipped the rest of the way to school. On the days when there *was* no Boris to love Robert usually got a kick or a punch.

The Harbournes had never allowed their children to have pets. They associated cats with hairs, dogs with noise and smells, and long walks at antisocial hours. But Robert pleaded so hard that they caved in and spent a large sum of money on a tank of tropical fish. It was installed in Billie's bedroom on gleaming white shelves and they showed him how much food to scatter in each time, how to check the water temperature and clear out the algae with a special net. There were bright green plastic plants in the tank and a hoop-shaped rock through which the fish could swim endlessly in and out.

Billie was interested for about twenty-four hours, then he got bored. He took to banging on the glass with his fists to liven things up, overfed the fish because he liked to watch them swim greedily up to the surface of the water and flop their mouths open. One day Robert went into the room and found that they were all dead. Billie had put sugar and salt in the water "to see what would happen." Dad emptied the tank, took it downstairs and put houseplants in it. There was no more talk of "pets."

And Billie got steadily worse. Three times his little suitcase was packed and put in the hall and they got as far as dialing the social worker, to ask her to remove him. Always, though, they hung up before anyone answered. That phone call meant that he would be automatically returned to the children's home and they couldn't do it to him. "It's got to get better," Mum said tearfully. Robert wasn't so sure.

One day, when they'd had Billie for about six weeks, Robert met mad Mrs. McCann from Dogs Rescue. She lived in a sprawling run-down bungalow near the canal and took in not only lost dogs and cats but had rabbits and hamsters, too. People said the place was overrun with wildlife. Sometimes she knocked on the Harbourne's door and held out a rusty tin, for her "work." She smelled strongly of cats and sweat and her clothes were so filthy and so full of holes they'd have been rejected for a jumble sale. Mum always gave her something, just to get rid of her. Afterward she sprayed all round with air freshener.

Mrs. McCann had a dog on a bit of rope. It was an extraordinary-looking creature, a bit labrador, a bit collie, a bit poodle. It had outsized ears and a lavatory-brush tail, a silky gold coat, a huge shaggy head, and melting brown eyes. She'd found it abandoned by the gates of the old slipper factory. I'll have to find a home for this one," she told Robert, "he's a terrible eater. Cruel what some people do to animals. Not looking for a dog, are you? Your mother

122

always supports my work."

"As matter of fact we are," said Robert.

"Well, what about this one then? He's not much more than a puppy and he's going to be a real beauty." Mrs. McCann's faded blue eyes grew round with love as she tickled the curious creature's ears while the lavatory-brush tail whirred like a propeller. "I've called him Prince," she said, "but of course you can choose your own name."

"Prince is fine," Robert told her, amazed at his own daring as he took the rope lead and fished in his pocket. "Er, I've only got 50p, Mrs. McCann. I don't get my paper-round money till Saturday."

"You keep it, sonny,' Mrs. McCann said magnanimously. "Buy him a tin of food with it."

By the end of the day Prince was installed in a big shed on the edge of some abandoned allotments, about a mile from home. It was a place Robert remembered from his early childhood, when Dad, who was a keen gardener, had been mad on growing prize vegetables. Nobody went there anymore and the nearest houses were far enough away not to be bothered by Prince's barking. Not that he made much noise, he was a placid sort of creature. For all his ugliness you looked into his great brown eyes and loved him on the spot.

For a few days Robert experimented, taking him for walks after his morning and evening paper rounds and slipping out of school at lunchtime to give him a quick run on the allotments. Then, one Friday afternoon, he brought Billie. He'd never deceived his parents before and this thing with Prince was big, *big*. But the minute he saw them together he knew that his instinct had been right. Billie immediately knelt down, flung his arms around the dog, and buried his face in the soft neck. Prince sniffed him all over then licked his face. The little boy laughed, tickled his stomach, then they were rolling over and over together, on the floor of the shed. Robert felt superfluous and, somehow, moved. He'd never seen Billie look happy before. His sharp little face had miraculously softened now and all the grown-up fear and suspicion had drained away.

It wasn't difficult to explain that for the time being Prince was a big secret and had to live in the shed. Billie was sharp as a needle and old for his years, he understood about Mum's pride in her house, that was why he'd ruined the carpet. He understood, too, about the need to deceive grown-ups. With his own parents he must have been constantly on his guard, Dad had said, keeping out of their way at the worst moments, ducking flying objects and dodging blows. The Prince secret was nothing compared with that. "Yeah, yeah, I get it," he said impatiently when Robert said they had to keep quiet. "But when can he come and live with us? I want him in my bedroom."

Robert began to make promises, hopeless he felt, at first, but as the days wore on and Billie's behavior at home and school improved dramatically, he began to think he really might be able to persuade his parents to have the dog at home. Since Prince had come into his life Billie had started to act like an ordinary eight-year-old boy. Just as long as he knew he could see the dog every day, play with him and take him for runs, he was happy. On the day Robert had to stay in bed with a stomach bug and nobody could go to the shed Billie went mad with frustration, pulled the cloth from under the dinner table and smashed all the crockery. But he never said a word about Prince. He trusted Robert now and he knew that the Harbournes mustn't be told yet.

The day after his bug Robert did tell them. He could see that the secret couldn't last forever and he'd proved that Prince was a big part of the answer to Billie's problems. But, anxious as they were to help, they wouldn't hear of having Prince. A big dog like that, they argued, was expensive to keep and a terrible tie, besides, they all led such busy lives. If Billie wasn't satisfied with something easy like fish, they told him gently, perhaps they'd buy him a rabbit. You could certainly stroke and cuddle those, they

were like dogs, really. Dad could make a special hutch for it, out in the garden.

That afternoon, when Robert went to the primary school to collect Billie, he wasn't there. He wasn't at the house either. He'd obviously slipped away just before home time, so nobody knew. He was missing for three days and nights during which Robert's parents were wracked by anguish and guilt. If only he'd come back, they said, he could have his precious dog. For all his problems they were growing to love him. The old shed was the first place they checked on but its door was open and Prince had gone. Billie's cardboard suitcase and the pathetic cache of "treasures" he had brought with him had gone too, from his room.

There were many "sightings" of Billie and Prince— down in the town, wandering along the bypass, in an amusement arcade in Bradford. Someone even said they thought they'd spotted a little boy with a dog climbing into a truck in a motorway service area near Northampton. It was terrible at home. Mr. Harbourne spent his evenings constructing an elaborate dog kennel. Mrs. Harbourne obsessively polished all the floors then started spring-cleaning her immaculate kitchen cupboards. Nobody spoke much but whenever the phone rang they all hurtled toward it. Sometimes it was the social services, sometimes the police. But nobody ever rang with news of Billie.

On the fourth day Mrs. McCann knocked on the door with her rusty money tin. Dad was down at the police station, begging them to hot up their search, Mum was asleep upstairs. She'd not been to bed for three nights. "I'm sorry, Mrs. McCann," Robert said, feeling in his pockets. "I've not got anything for you today."

"That little boy of yours," she said, thrusting her big crumpled face right up to him and letting out a blast of foul breath, "he's been by the canal, I saw him this morning. Shouldn't be wandering around on his own like that, you know. It's dangerous that canal, the dog might pull him in.

126

Our Cissie's kiddie..." But Robert didn't wait to listen to any more. He pushed past her, pulled his bike out of the garage and pedaled off toward the allotments. It was getting dark and he'd not stopped to put the lights on. In the town center a policeman hollered at him to stop, but he took no notice.

Billie was in the shed with Prince and they were both fast asleep. The child lay curled around inside the curve of the pale gold belly of the dog, his head pillowed against its softness, one hand around the neck. Prince was making little snoring noises and a large paw was stretched across Billie's body as if to say, "Don't touch, this is my friend." At Billie's feet was the little cardboard case. On top, neatly arranged, were all the precious animal postcards that Robert had given him. As he looked at Billie and Prince his eyes filled with sudden tears. He'd once read about a famous explorer going to sleep in the presence of a lion. The lion had also slept, a sleep, he had written, that must surely be the ultimate act of trust.

They kept Prince and they kept Billie. The funny-looking dog filled out and eventually grew into its ears and into its extraordinary tail. It loved living with the Harbournes and as the months passed it became big and brave and lovely. Billie did too.

LUCKY LIPS

PAUL JENNINGS

MARCUS FELT SILLY. He was embarrassed. But he knocked on the door anyway. There was no answer from inside the dark house. It was as silent as the grave. Then he noticed a movement behind the curtain; someone was watching him. He could see a dark eye peering through a chink in the curtain. There was a rustling noise inside that sounded like rats' feet on a bare floor.

The door slowly opened and Ma Scritchet's face appeared. It was true what people said—she looked like a witch. She had hair like straw and her nose was hooked and long. She smiled showing pointed, yellow teeth.

"Come in," she said. "I have been waiting for you."

Marcus was not going to let this old woman fool him. "How could you be expecting me?" he answered. "No one knew I was coming here." He felt better now. He could see that it was all a trick. She was a faker. A phony. Did she really expect him to believe that she knew he was coming?

"I knew you were coming," she said. "And I know *why* you have come."

128

This time Marcus knew she was lying. He had not told anyone about his problem. There was not one person in the world that knew about it, it was too embarrassing. The other kids would laugh if they knew.

He decided to go home. But first he would stir this old bag up a bit. "Okay, Ma," he said. "Why have I come?"

She looked him straight in the eye. "You are sixteen years old," she told him. "And you have never been kissed."

Marcus could feel his face turning red. He was blushing. She knew—she knew all about it. She must be able to read minds. The stories that were told about her must be true. He felt silly and small, and he didn't know what to do.

Ma Scritchet started to laugh, a long cackling laugh. It made Marcus shiver. "Come with me," she said. She led him along a dark, narrow passage and up some wooden stairs. The house was filled with junk: broken TV sets and old bicycles, piles of books and empty bottles. The stair rails were covered in cobwebs. They went into a small room at the top of the house.

Inside the room was a couch and a chair. Nothing else. It was not what Marcus had expected. He thought there would be a crystal ball on a round table and lots of junk and equipment for telling fortunes. The room was almost bare.

Ma Scritchet held out her hand. "This will cost you twenty dollars," she said to Marcus.

"I pay after, not before," said Marcus. "This could be a trick."

"You pay before, not after," said Ma Scritchet. "I only help those that believe in me." Marcus looked into her eyes. They were cold and hard. He took out his wallet and gave her twenty dollars, and she tucked it inside her dress. Then she said, "Lie down on the couch."

Marcus lay on the couch and stared at the ceiling. A tiny spider was spinning a web in the corner. Marcus felt foolish lying there on a couch in this old woman's house.

He wished he hadn't come; he wanted to go home. But
there was something about Ma Scritchet that made him
nervous. And now that he had paid his twenty dollars he
was going to get his money's worth. "Well," he said. "I
suppose that you want me to tell you about my problem."

"No," said Ma Scritchet. "I will tell you about it. You just
stay there and listen." Marcus did as she said.

"You have never kissed a girl," said the old woman in a
low voice. "You have tried plenty of times. But they always
turn you down. They think you are stuck up and selfish.
They don't like the things you say about other people.
Some girls go out with you once, but when you get home to
their front door they always say, 'Thank you' and go
inside."

Marcus listened in silence. Most of it was true. He knew
he wasn't stuck up and selfish, but the rest of it was right.
He tried everything he could think of. He would take a girl
to the movies and buy her chocolates. He would even pay
for her to get in. But then, right at the end when they were
saying "good night," he would close his eyes, pucker up
his lips and lean forward, to find himself kissing the closed

front door of the girl's house. It was maddening. It was enough to make him spit. And it had happened dozens of times. Not one girl would give him a kiss.

"Well," said Marcus to Ma Scritchet. "Can you help me? That's what I gave you the twenty dollars for."

She smiled but said nothing. It was not a nice smile. It was a smile that made Marcus feel foolish. She stood up without a word and left the room, and Marcus could hear her footsteps clipping down the stairs. A minute or so later he heard her coming back. She came into the room and held out a small tube. "Take this," she said. "It's just what you need. This will do the trick."

Marcus took it out of her hand and looked at it. It was a stick of lipstick in a small gold container. "I'm not wearing lipstick," Marcus told her. "You must think I'm crazy." He sat up and jumped off the couch. This had gone far enough. He wondered if he could get his money back.

"Sit down, boy," said Ma Scritchet in a cold voice. "And listen to me. You put that on your lips and you will get all the kisses you want. It has no color. It's clear and no one will be able to see it. But it will do the trick. It will work on any female. Just put some of that on your lips and the nearest girl will want to kiss you."

Marcus looked at the tube of lipstick. He didn't know whether to believe it or not. It might work. Old Ma Scritchet could read his mind; she knew what his problem was without being told. This lipstick could be just what he needed. "Okay," he said. "I'll give it a try. But it had better work. If it doesn't, I will be back for my twenty dollars."

"It will work," hissed Ma Scritchet. "It will work better than you think. Now it's time for you to go. The session is over." She led Marcus down the narrow stairs and along the passage to the front door. He stepped out into the sunlight. It was bright and made him blink. As Ma Scritchet closed the door she told Marcus one more thing. "This lipstick will only work once on each person. One girl: one kiss. That's the way it works."

She closed the door in his face without saying another thing. Once more the old house was quiet.

Marcus kept the lipstick for a week before he used it. When he got home to his room with his record player and the posters on the wall, the whole thing seemed like a dream. The old house and Ma Scritchet were from another world. He wondered whether or not the visit had really happened, but he had the lipstick to prove that it had.

He held it in his hand. It had a strange appearance and he found that it glowed in the dark. He put it in a drawer and left it there.

Later that week a new girl started at Marcus's school. Her name was Jill. Marcus didn't waste any time; he asked her out for a date on her first day at school. She didn't seem too keen about going with him, but she was shy and didn't want to seem unfriendly, especially as she didn't know anyone at the school. In the end she agreed to go to a disco with him on Friday night.

Marcus arranged to meet Jill inside the disco. That way he wouldn't have to pay for her to get in. It wasn't a bad turn and Jill seemed to enjoy it. As he danced Marcus could feel the lipstick in his pocket. He couldn't forget about it; it annoyed him. It was like having a stone in his shoe.

At eleven o'clock they decided to go home. It was only a short walk back to Jill's house. As they walked, Jill chatted happily; she was glad that she had made a new friend so quickly. Marcus started to feel a bit guilty. He fingered the lipstick in his pocket. Should he use it? He remembered something about stolen kisses. Was he stealing a kiss if he used the lipstick? Not really—if it worked Jill would be kissing him of her own free will. Anyway, it probably wouldn't work. Old Ma Scritchet had probably played a trick on him. He would never know unless he tried it. He just had to know if the lipstick worked, and this was his big chance.

As they went inside the front gate of Jill's house, Marcus

132

pretended to bend down and do up his shoelace. He quickly pulled out the lipstick and smeared some on his lips. Then he stood up. His lips were tingling. He noticed that Jill was looking at him in a strange way; her eyes were wide open and staring. Then she rushed forward, threw her arms around Marcus's neck and kissed him. Marcus was so surprised that he nearly fell over.

Jill jumped back as if she had been burned. She put her hand up to her mouth and went red in the face. "I, I, I'm sorry, Marcus. I don't know what came over me. What must you think of me? I've never done anything like that before."

"Don't worry about it. That sort of thing happens to me all the time. The girls find me irresistible."

Jill didn't know what to say. She was blushing. She couldn't understand what had happened. "I'd better go in," she said. "I'm really sorry. I didn't mean to do that." Then she turned around and rushed into the house.

Marcus whistled to himself as he walked home. "It works," he thought. "The lipstick really works." He couldn't wait to try it on someone else.

It was not so easy for Marcus to find his next victim. None of the girls at school wanted to go out with him. It was no use asking Jill again, as the lipstick only worked once on each person. He asked ten girls to go to the movies with him and they all said "no."

He started to get cross. "Stuck up snobs," he said to himself. "I'll teach them a lesson." He decided to make the most popular girl in the school kiss him. That would show them all. Her name was Fay Billings.

The trouble was that he knew she wouldn't go out on a date with him. Then he had a bright idea: he wouldn't even bother about a date. He would just go around to Fay's house and ask to see her. He would put the lipstick on before he arrived, and when she came to the door she would give him a big kiss. The news would soon get around and the other kids would think he had something good going. It would make him popular with the girls.

Marcus grinned. It was a great idea. He decided to put it into action straightaway. He rode his bike around to Fay's house and leaned it against the fence. Then he took out the lipstick and put some on his lips. He walked up to the front door and rang the bell with a big smile on his face.

No one answered the door. He could hear a vacuum cleaner going inside so he rang the bell again. The sound of the vacuum cleaner stopped and Mrs. Billings appeared at the door. She had a towel wrapped around her head and had dust on her face from the housework she had been doing. She had never seen Marcus before; he was not one of Fay's friends.

Mrs. Billings was just going to ask Marcus what he wanted when a strange look came over her face. Her eyes went large and round. They looked as if they were going to pop out. Then she threw her arms around Marcus's neck and kissed him on the mouth.

It was hard to say who was more surprised, Marcus or Mrs. Billings. They sprang apart and looked around to see if anyone had seen what happened. Marcus didn't want anyone to see him being kissed by a forty-year-old woman. How embarrassing. "My goodness," said Mrs. Billings. "What am I doing? Kissing a perfect stranger. And you're so young. What has got into me? What would my husband think? Please excuse me. I must be ill. I think I had better go and have a little rest." She turned around and walked slowly into the house. She shook her head as she went.

Marcus rode home slowly. He was not pleased. This was not working out the way he wanted. What if someone had seen him being kissed by an old lady like Mrs. Billings? He would never live it down. He had had the lipstick for two weeks now and had only received one decent kiss. None of the girls would go out with him. And he couldn't wear the lipstick just anywhere—he didn't want any other mothers kissing him.

He decided to make Fay Billings kiss him at school, in front of all the other kids. That would show them that he had something special. All the girls would be chasing him after that. He would be the most popular boy in the school.

He picked his moment carefully. He sat next to Fay for the Math lesson the next day. She looked at him with a funny expression on her face but she didn't say anything. Miss White was late for the class. She was a young teacher and was popular with the students, but she was always late. This was the chance that Marcus had been waiting for. He bent down under the desk and put on some of the lipstick. Then he sat up in the desk and looked at Fay.

The lipstick worked. Fay's eyes went round and she threw herself on to Marcus and kissed him. Then she jumped back and gave a little cry. Marcus looked around with a grin on his face, but it did not last for long. All the girls' eyes were wide and staring. Tissy came up and kissed him. And then Gerda and Helen and Betty and Maria. They climbed over each other in the rush to get to him.

135

They shrieked and screamed and fought; they scratched and fought and bit. Marcus fell onto the floor under a struggling, squirming heap of girls.

When all the sixteen girls in the class had kissed him there was silence. They were in a state of shock—they couldn't understand what had happened. They just sat there looking at each other. Marcus had his tie ripped off and his shirt was torn. He had a cut lip and a black eye.

Then Gerda yelled out, "I kissed Marcus! Arrgghh . . ." She rushed over to the tap and started washing her mouth out. All the girls started wiping their mouths as if they had eaten something nasty. Then everybody started laughing. The boys laughed, and the girls laughed. They rolled around the floor holding their sides. Tears rolled out of their eyes. Everybody laughed, except Marcus.

He knew that they were laughing at him. And he didn't think that it was funny.

After all the kissing at school everyone called Marcus "Lucky Lips." Nobody liked Marcus any better than before and the girls still stayed away from him. Everyone talked about the kissing session for a while; then they forgot about it and talked about other things. But Marcus didn't forget about it. He felt like a fool. Everyone had laughed at him. He was worse off now than he had been before.

He thought about taking the lipstick back to Ma Scritchet and telling her what he thought about it, but he was too scared. There was something creepy about that old lady and he didn't really want to see her.

Marcus didn't use the lipstick again for about a month. None of the girls would go out with him and he wasn't going to risk wearing it just anywhere. Not after what happened at school that day. But he always carried the lipstick with him, just in case.

The last time he used it was at the Royal Melbourne Show. The whole class at school went there on an excursion. They had to collect material for an assignment. Marcus and Fay Billings and two other boys walked around together. They didn't really want Marcus with them: they thought he was a show-off. But they let him tag along. They didn't want to hurt his feelings.

The favorite spots at the show were the sideshows. There were knock-em-downs and rides on the Mad Mouse. There was a fat lady and a mirror maze. There was a ghost train and dozens of other rides. One of the side shows had a sign up saying "BIG BEN THE STRONGEST MAN IN THE WORLD."

They all milled around looking at the tent. It was close to one of the animal pavilions. There was a great hall full of pigs nearby. "Let's go and look at the pigs," said Fay.

"No," answered Marcus. "Who wants to look at filthy pigs. Let's go and see Big Ben. He fights people. Anyone who can beat him wins one thousand dollars and gets to kiss the Queen Of The Show."

"That would be just the thing for Lucky Lips," said Fay.

They all laughed, except Marcus. He went red in the face.

"I could get a kiss from the Queen Of The Show," he said. They all laughed again. "All right," said Marcus. "Just watch me." He paid his dollar and went inside Big Ben's tent. The others all followed him; they wanted to see what was going to happen.

Inside the tent was a boxing ring. Big Ben was standing inside it waiting for someone to fight him and try to win the thousand dollars and a kiss from the Queen Of The Show. She sat on a high chair behind the ring. Marcus looked at her. She was beautiful; he wouldn't mind a kiss from her. Then he looked at Big Ben. He was the biggest man Marcus had ever seen. He had huge muscles and was covered in tattoos. And he looked mean—very mean.

Marcus ducked around the ring to where the Queen Of The Show sat. He quickly put on some of the invisible lipstick, and at once the beauty queen jumped off her chair and kissed Marcus. Everyone laughed except Big Ben. He roared in fury. "Trying to steal a kiss without a fight, are you?" he yelled. "I'll teach you a lesson, my boy."

Marcus tried to run away but he was not quick enough. Big Ben grabbed him and lifted Marcus high into the air. Then he walked outside the tent and across to the pig pavilion. Marcus wriggled and yelled, but it was no good; he couldn't get away. Big Ben carried Marcus over to one of the pig pens and threw him inside.

Marcus crashed to the floor of the pen. He felt dizzy. The world seemed to be spinning around. He tried to stand up, but he couldn't. The floor was covered in foul smelling muck. In the corner Marcus could see the biggest pig that he had ever seen. It was eating rotten vegetables and slops from a trough. It was dribbling and slobbering as it ate. Its teeth were green. It turned around and looked at Marcus. It was a sow.

Marcus suddenly remembered something that Ma Scritchet had said about the lipstick. She had said: "It will work on any female." Marcus started to scream. "Get me out. Get me out."

But it was too late. The sow came over for her kiss.

A STAR FOR THE LATECOMER

PAUL ZINDEL AND BONNIE ZINDEL

O N SATURDAY MORNING I opened my eyes and ran to the window and saw the weather was being kind; just a few clouds—it was a beautiful sky. The smell of Southern fried chicken was winding its way up the staircase already, and I knew that my mother was busy over the stove, crushing the cornflakes, breading the chicken and dipping it into oil to cook it for my picnic basket. That simple smell of cooking chicken so early in the morning I took as my mother's absolute approval of my date; but more important, she must be feeling good today. Deep down I knew she was romantic even though she didn't live her own life that way. Maybe that's why she got so excited about my romantic escapades. She had no objection to romance as long as it wouldn't interfere with my career.

"Good morning, Mom," I said, giving her a kiss as I came into the kitchen.

"Good morning, Brooke," she said, giving me a quick hug and snapping a pair of tongs like she was catching tsetse flies. "Were you able to sleep?" she asked with a twinkle.

"Yes," I said. "The chicken looks delicious."

"I'm making twelve pieces, just in case he's got a big appetite. If it's too much you can throw it overboard for the seagulls."

"How do you feel this morning?" I asked, watching for what went unspoken.

"This morning I woke up feeling better than I have all week."

"Don't overdo it," I said, trying to take the tongs from her.

"No, I'm really enjoying it," she said, and I believed her.

My mother already had a lovely straw basket out on the counter and an old red-checked tablecloth that we never used except on evenings when my mother made a typically authentic American-Italian dinner, which meant spaghetti with Ragu sauce.

"I almost forgot napkins," she said as she ran to the hatch in the dining room and pulled out two red linen cloths.

"Wow, you're certainly making quite a picnic for us," I said, overwhelmed. "Thanks."

"I like doing it," she said. "I'm putting in two glasses, but you can buy the Coke later so it's cold."

"Okay, Mom."

"Now, I want you to use your head on this boat trip," my mother started more seriously. "Don't do anything foolish like jumping into the Sound because it looks good. There are sharks out there, and remember it's October and the water's got a chill to it already. I don't want you catching a cold."

"No jumping in the Sound."

"You're a smart girl, Brooke. I know you'll take care of yourself."

I took a spoon and started scooping out some of the fried cornflakes that never made it onto the chicken. The crunchy texture and zesty fried flavor gave the cereal a new dimension. As I was scraping around the sides of the

141

hot pan for the last morsels, my thoughts drifted to Brandon.

"Do you think Brandon likes me a little?" I asked, searching for some assurance.

"He wouldn't ask you out if he hated you," she said, laughing.

"But I wonder in what way he likes me? As a friend? Or do you think he could like me more?"

"I think he likes you more."

"He smiles a lot at me and does try to sit next to me sometimes. During our last fire drill he touched the embroidery on the back of my shirt trying to figure out if it was a bird or a deer."

"Some boys are shy at first until they know the girl likes them. Boys like to play it safe, take the cue from the girl."

"What if I give the cue and he doesn't take it? I'd feel like an idiot."

"Be yourself, sweetheart. You like him, don't hide it. Don't play games. Don't jump on him, but don't play games. I know you see the difference."

Don't play games rang in my ears. Don't play games.

The drive to Brandon's country house was beautiful. My mother was still able to maneuver the car through traffic just like always. And as she drove she wasn't aware that I was staring at her. She really looked beautiful and springlike for this Indian summer day. Her nails were freshly done in a pink that picked up a touch of pink in her white-flowered dress. It reminded me of field upon field of anemones. I thought she had decided to wear it today because, as she had said when she bought it, "This is an 'up' dress. It reminds me of sunshine and makes me feel enthusiastic." That was her, all right. She was always enthusiastic. I was proud of the way she looked. Then I put my head toward the window to look at myself in the outside mirror to see if I looked as pretty as she did at that moment.

The directions Brandon's mother had given her the night

before were very easy to follow.

"Here we are," my mother said, pulling up in front of a modest Cape Cod house.

I was relieved that it wasn't too big a home. Brandon saw us arrive and was at the front door before we could ring the bell.

"Hi, Brooke," he said, and he really looked happy to see me. "Hello, Mrs. Hillary," he said to my mother, making her feel very welcome. Brandon had his usual relaxed smile and there was something different about seeing him in this country setting. He seemed even more natural, more ordinary, not a rich-kid actor about to go out to Hollywood to be in a movie.

His home had modern furniture: a few chrome tables and a hanging lamp suspended from the middle of the room, a couple of leather sofas and beyond that some large glass windows leading on to a patio with white wrought iron furniture. His mother came over immediately and warmly greeted us, putting my mother and me even more at ease. She appeared very sophisticated and worldly and gracious. As she walked toward us, I noticed a similarity between Brandon and his mother, especially around the eyes.

"Hello, Brooke," she said. "And *Claire*, how are you?" she asked my mother, extending her hand. "You're looking wonderful."

"Thank you," my mother said. "It was very lovely of you to invite me."

I must say that even though Brandon's mother knew about my Mom's illness, there was no trace of discomfort or awkwardness as they talked. I saw they would get along just fine. "Let's drop the kids off at the boat, then you and I can get ourselves a nice lobster salad at the club," Brandon's mother said, ushering us out to the car. Brandon's mother put her arm in my mother's and Brandon gave me a big wink as he picked up my picnic basket.

"Wow, what a lunch," he said, quite pleased. "It looks terrific."

"Thank you," I said, smiling to my mother, knowing that the compliment was certainly hers and not mine.

We waved good-bye to our mothers at the club and walked down to the main dock. There were hundreds of boats. Fishing boats, white yachts, little sailboats, some already rigged and heading out over the sparkling wave tips. "Most people don't like taking their boats out of the water," Brandon told me. "We hate to admit summer's over, but I'm afraid this will be my last ride of the season."

"What happens to your boat for the winter?" I wondered.

"It goes into hibernation; that's why this ride is so special and I thought you'd enjoy it."

I couldn't tell if he meant that romantically or maybe he just thought I liked water a whole lot, which I really don't. We passed people working on their boats as we made our way to the end of the pier.

"There she is," he said, proudly.

In front of us was a small fiberglass speedboat, and on it was painted the word *Apocalypse*.

"The *Apocalypse*?" I questioned.

"Yes," Brandon said, "my father gave it that name."

"What does it mean?" I asked.

"It's biblical—some kind of a big disaster."

"Sounds like the wrong name for a boat," I remarked.

144

"Yeah," he agreed, "I think it's the wrong name for anything."

He helped me into the boat and handed me the basket while he untied the mooring ropes from the pier. He got in, pushed us away from the dock and pulled the cord to start the outboard. The engine sputtered a few times, but then it roared. He moved some levers, then yelled, "Hold on," while the craft leaped forward.

When we were about a quarter of a mile from the shore, he said, "Here, you want to steer the boat?"

"Great," I cried out, never having done it before. A few sprays of water went in our faces and I was thankful I was wearing a red windbreaker.

"You seem right at home on the high seas," he said.

"Thanks," I accepted. "I have to admit, though, I'm an earth person. I feel safer on land."

"I'm a water person for sure," he said. "In fact, that's my dream one day—I want to charter a large sailing ship and cross the Atlantic." He put his hand on top of mine to help me turn the engine slightly, and his touch was so wonderful I hoped he would never let go. The boat followed in an arc, and then he lifted his hand to point off to the right. "See that island over there? The one with the inlet and small beach?" I shielded my eyes and saw a stub of shining sand broken by clusters of wild plum trees and low green shrubs.

"Yes," I said.

"That's where we'll have our picnic. Right in the cove."

"Is that where you go to be alone?" I asked.

"Also when I'm happy." He grinned.

Within a few minutes he pushed the boat up on shore. I took off my shoes and we both walked around a few large rocks to get to the beach. Brandon put down a blanket, on which I placed the basket.

"Come on," he said, "let me show you around my island."

He took me by the hand and we ran through the sand

145

until we reached a part of the beach covered with unusual shells. The tide had gone out and left a beautiful collection.

"Look," I said, "this one's perfect." I lifted a large conch shell. It was twisted, the kind you're supposed to put to your ear and listen to for the ocean.

"Listen," I said, as I put it to his ear. "I think this shell

knows all your secrets."

He listened intently for a second. "Don't believe it." He shook his head. "This shell is bonkers."

We both burst into laughter again.

"Look at this one," he said, picking up a brown-and-white shell and putting it to my ear. I closed my eyes and tried listening.

"This is my kind of conch," he said.

"Is it?" I asked.

"The sea talks," he replied.

"What does it say?"

"Can't figure that out." He laughed and I laughed with him. He held the shell out for me and I took it. My hand touched his for a moment and I slipped the shell into the pocket of my shorts.

For hours we laughed and ran and felt free. We built a sandcastle until the tide started to come forward and take it back. We brushed the drying sand from each other's backs. Then we picked some ripe red plums. The whole afternoon was going by too quickly.

"I'm famished," Brandon said.

"Chow's on," I yelled. "Last one back to the blanket is a wet fish." I lost the race, but I really didn't try to win. We ate almost all the chicken, as well as the potato chips. Brandon opened the bottles of Coke we'd picked up at the club and I offered him a choice between shortbread and chocolate chip cookies. We were so full that we just collapsed on the blanket. We didn't have enough energy to talk; we just looked straight up at the sun and closed our eyes, and we both fell asleep for a few moments. We were so quiet, it was as if we knew we didn't have to say a word to each other. I had never felt so close to another person in my life. He reached over and took my hand and then swung around, resting his head on my lap. I sat up, trying not to show how nervous and happy I was, but then I reached down and stroked his soft blond hair that fell into a few curls around his face. He closed his eyes and stretched and started to hum and moved my fingers to his lips. We listened to the waves breaking. Then, slowly, he reached both hands up and pulled me down to kiss him. We were together for hours but it seemed like minutes, and before I knew it I opened my eyes and saw him backlighted by streaks of yellow and purple tossed across the sky.

"Look," I said, "the sun is starting to set. Do you know what time it is?"

"I didn't bring a watch," Brandon said.

"I don't have one either but I told my mother I'd be back by six."

"I can guess the time," Brandon said, "from the position of the sun. I'm sure it's past five-thirty."

"Maybe we should start back," I suggested.

"I suppose you're right," he said, kissing me again. Then we just looked at each other and I understood why some people can feel so happy they want to cry.

We threw everything onto the blanket and grabbed it so that it looked like we were carrying a dead man back to the boat. We swung it in, but before pushing the boat off Brandon stuck out his toe and wrote in the sand three large numbers, a 1, a 4, and a 3.

"One-four-three?" I inquired. "What does that mean?"

"It's a code. It means *I love you*."

"How can one-four-three mean I love you?"

"It's the number of letters in each word."

I sat there silently figuring it out in my mind.

"Oh," was all I could say. I didn't know whether he felt the way I did or was just telling me a mathematical equation. I wanted to believe that he was saying what I felt, too.

We stared into each other's eyes again. My heart soared like a bird finding its way home. I knew what it was to feel complete. *Don't play games*. It felt wonderful, I thought, then found myself whispering back, "One-four-three."

Brandon reached out and took my hand and smiled a smile I had never seen before, a smile that made me feel it was coming from a deeper place, beyond school, beyond Rudley's, beyond words. I felt his smile came right from his soul as though we had made a spiritual connection with each other. I had to break the intensity of the moment because it reached a new kind of pain for me—the one

148

called happiness.

"I don't want my mother to worry about me," I said.

"Of course. I'm sorry," he said. We jumped into the boat and raced back out into the Sound. "The trip home is only about a half hour. Don't worry," he yelled over the roar of the motor.

"I won't," I said.

The water was calm and the sun was going down quickly. The yellows and purples of the sky were now darker, and clouds strung themselves along the horizon like sentries.

"Twilight is my favorite time of the day," I said.

"Why?" he asked.

"I feel it shows the world in its purest colors."

"I like dawn," he announced, "because I never know what it will bring."

It seemed as if almost half an hour had gone by, but I didn't see any land. It had become quite dark and the stars had come out.

"Brandon," I asked, over the noise of the pistons clanking and water churning, "did you take me out because you felt sorry for me?"

Brandon looked taken aback.

"I'm not a social worker," he said, looking right into my eyes.

"I'm sorry," I confessed. "It's hard for me to believe in anything good happening to me since I found out my mother was dying."

He shut off the motor and the boat began to drift. "I asked you out because I like you," he said, and I remembered 1-4-3 in the sand.

"I wanted to make sure," I said.

He reached out and took my hand. "You can be sure," he said firmly.

"I'm afraid, Brandon. Afraid of losing my mother. Afraid of being alone."

Brandon held me. "You won't be alone, Brooke."

"I'm afraid that anything I care about will die. I'm afraid of marriage and children. I'm afraid if I love my husband and children, they will die, too."

"Brooke, don't be afraid," he said putting his arm around me. "This is a hard time for you."

"Brandon, I have never seen anyone die. Have you?" He shook his head no.

"Are you afraid to die?" I asked him.

"No," he said. "I feel impervious to death. Sometimes I like speeding along an empty road at ninety miles per hour. Brooke, all of life is a gamble. It's that gamble that makes me feel alive. If I didn't take chances I'd be a big blob. Do you think it'll be easy for me to go out to Hollywood and face the cameras every day? I'm scared to death. But I'm going to do it. The picture might be awful. People might sit there and say that guy can't act for beans, but I'm going to gamble on it because I want big stakes in life. And so do you. Watch out," he said, standing up to start the engine again. He pulled the cord a few times and it wouldn't start. He pulled it again.

"What's wrong?" I asked.

"I'll have to let it rest a minute," he said. "I don't want to flood the engine."

After a few minutes, he pulled again and again and again on the cord. He stooped down, leaned over and pulled out the gas tank. I could tell from the way it rattled it was empty. He grabbed quickly for the reserve tank. We were stuck out there with two empty gas tanks!

"What will we do?" I asked, thinking of my mother worrying.

"Nothing—it'll be all right," he said. "Somebody must have taken this boat out and drained the reserve. They rip everything off nowadays. Sometimes they rip stuff off, then they bring it back."

"I'm not a good swimmer," I confessed. "I panic if my head goes underwater."

"How are you on the back float?"

"That's my best," I said.

"Look, don't worry, we'll sit here and wait for someone to pass by and give us a tow."

I looked around. By now it was getting dark and cold.

"A boat should be coming soon," Brandon said. "We're only a few minutes away. Don't worry, your mother won't be waiting long."

During the next fifteen minutes it got even colder, and the night air surrounded us as we drifted aimlessly into nowhere. Brandon was getting nervous but he took off his sweater and helped me slip it on. It was warm from him and I felt protected. Now it was so dark you could hardly see anything except the beacon from a lighthouse miles away. After what seemed like hours, we heard the sound of a motorboat. Brandon and I both cupped our hands.

"Help, we're out of gas! Help! Help!"

"Do you think someone heard?" I asked.

"I can't tell," he said. "We'll see soon enough."

Then we didn't hear anything.

"Help! Help!" we screamed together again into the night. I could see my mother's face. She'd be very, very frightened.

Suddenly we heard the sound of a boat coming in our direction.

"One, two, three," Brandon directed, and we yelled together again. "*Help, this way, here we are!*"

A beam of light shot in our direction and a small fishing boat pulled up next to us. An old rugged-looking fisherman with whiskers stood up in his boat. "What are you kids doing out on the Sound at this hour?" he scolded.

"My motor's gone," Brandon said. "I'm out of gas!"

"You're kidding." He laughed. "Usually when a boy takes a girl out and runs out of gas, it's in a car and it's deliberate. Here, pull up," the fisherman ordered. "I'll give you a tow."

The man threw a rope at Brandon, who tied it to the front of the boat and sat down next to me. "Hold on tight," he whispered. "We'll be home in a few minutes now. I'm sorry," he said, squeezing my hand.

When we reached the dock, several people stood under a light. My mother was in the front and she looked drained. Brandon's mother was close beside her. Both of them talked so fast it all became one long run-on sentence. *"We thought you got lost at sea we called the Coast Guard we called everybody what do you mean you ran out of gas what do you mean the motor conked out where were you what did you do Brooke, you really scared me Brooke, why did you do that Brooke, you knew it was getting dark."*

"I'm sorry, I'm sorry," I kept repeating as someone wrapped a blanket around me and headed me toward a car. It was as though Brandon and I were being separated by all these people and our mothers talking so fast; *why this? why that?* But all I heard was a voice inside of me saying, *Hey, Brooke, what happened today is the most important thing in your life. What happened is more life-giving and exciting and electric than anything on any stage in the world.* I wanted Brandon's love more than anything in the universe. More than dancing, or applause, or anything! Maybe we were gambling for different stakes. He wanted success, but maybe he wanted the same stakes as I did when it came to us. Yes, I told myself. He does feel something for me. He does love me. I mean something to him and this time I have a chance. *This is what I want out of life*, I wanted to cry out. *This!* And without it I would die.

THE PLATE:
A QUESTION OF VALUES

GERALDINE McCAUGHREAN

This story comes from A Pack of Lies, *a novel about an antique shop romance between Ailsa, daughter of the owner, and a mysterious young man called M. C. C. Berkshire. Through him she discovers that everything in the shop has a story behind it, including an old blue plate . . .*

O F THE HUNDRED POUNDS nothing remained. Other larger purchases M. C. C. Berkshire had made at the car boot sale and flea market arrived later in the day: a set of bookshelves and a stuffed salmon in a glass case. The little shop seemed to groan at the prospect of swallowing yet more indigestible junk, and if it had not been for the sale of the clock, the bookshelves would never have found a piece of wall to lean their backs against.

Mrs. Povey said to her daughter, "Maybe he's right to open up the book side of the business."

But when a teacher from Ailsa's school came in one day and thumbed his way through the fiction, he was brought gradually to a halt and a shiver by the feeling that someone was watching him. He looked up, and found M. C. C. Berkshire standing a word's length away from him, scowling. The teacher rummaged for his wallet. But M. C. C.

said, "I haven't read those yet," and prised the books out of the customer's hand. "I've been saving the fiction, you see."

"Ah! Quite!" exclaimed the teacher, and turned tail and fled, casting a look of bewildered pity at Ailsa and Mrs. Povey. (The word got about school after that, that Ailsa had a strange, deranged brother at home and that he was the reason the shop was in such dire financial trouble.)

"*That's* how to sell a thing," said Ailsa sarcastically, when her teacher was gone. Then Berkshire looked down at the books cradled against his stomach and stroked the spines with his fingers and seemed too ashamed to speak. And Ailsa wished she had kept silent, and wondered what had possessed her to be so rude. "It doesn't matter," she said. "Books don't pay enough to make any difference. They're not worth anything. Mum sells them for pennies, second-hand books."

"Some are worth hundreds!" said M. C. C., perking up.

"We don't have any like that."

"It's all a question of values," he said, appraising his new bookshelves, full of dilapidated paperbacks, and his eyes when he said it were as deep as Chancery, full of glints of gold from the lamplight. "Money isn't everything."

The sky outside was almost black with rain and every car that went by had its lamps switched on. With a loud crack, a thundercloud broke overhead. Two lovers, joined at the hands like Siamese twins, came bursting into the shop, laughing, and shaking off the rain. It was plain they had dashed into the first handy shelter and had no intention of buying.

"Oh, this is pretty . . . Oo, look at that dear little vase . . . what a pity this has lost its lid," said the girl from time to time. But her boyfriend was only watching for the rain to go off. She picked up a little book of Chinese folktales lying open on the *chaise longue*. When she lifted her eyes from browsing through it, she found herself being watched, from the dark recesses of the shop, by a young man.

155

M. C. C. pressed the palms of his hands together and bowed from the waist. He moved silently round the *chaise longue* and took the book out of her hands as if to read its title. "Ah! You are interested in ancient China, then!" She recoiled in alarm. "In that case, permit me to draw your attention to this charming plate."

"Oh look, Brian! What a pretty plate!" cried the girl, dubiously. M. C. C. slyly slipped the book into his pocket.

Brian came and looked at the blue and white plate balanced between two urns. "Oh yeah. Willow Pattern. Your Gran's got a whole service like it. Is that the only one?"

It was the only one—and even so, Ailsa could not remember seeing it before, though she knew the kind of thing. Well, the Willow Pattern is a common enough design.

"Is it old?" asked the girl, looking for a price.

"The story is," said M. C. C. Berkshire . . .

156

Long ago, in China, during the Ch'ing dynasty and the days of the Manchu Emperor Ch'ien Lung, there lived a potter called Ho Pa. He was a mean, greedy and spiteful man. But he had an apprentice working for him whose work was so perfect that people called from far and near to buy porcelain at Ho Pa's pottery. Ho Pa grew very rich indeed. But he did not pay any of the money to the apprentice, Wa Fan, who did all the work. Instead, he cursed and cuffed the young man and made his life miserable and called his pottery worthless and ugly.

If only Wa Fan had known! His beautiful vases and plates and teapots and dishes were bought even by the Emperor's Court! And travelers from far distant lands paid huge sums to sail away with just one piece of Wa Fan's craftsmanship. One pattern they asked for more often than any other. "Give us Willow-Pattern plates, Ho Pa! We will pay you extra if you make us Willow-Pattern china in blue and white!"

Then Ho Pa would stick his head round the door of the hot, wet pottery and shout, "Willow Pattern, Wa Fan! Give me more Willow Pattern, you idle son of a sleeping dog!"

Wa Fan did not mind. The Willow Pattern is a very beautiful pattern and tells the love story of a boy and a girl and a garden, and Wa Fan delighted in painting (in blue glaze with a very fine brush) the pretty garden with its bridge and pagodas. He painted petals onto the chrysanthemums with such care that the flowers seemed to be alive. He painted the figures so beautifully that their clothes seemed to billow in the breeze.

Sometimes—on the best days of all—his master's daughter, Liu, would come into the pottery and talk to him about his work and admire the china drying on the racks. She never tired of hearing Wa Fan tell her the story of the Willow Pattern, as she pointed out each detail in turn.

"And who is this?" she would ask (although she already knew).

"That is the cruel father," said Wa Fan. "A rich merchant

157

who will not let his lovely daughter marry the gardener."

"And this is the lovely daughter?" Liu would say, (although, of course, she already knew). "And this is the poor gardener? What became of the unhappy lovers?"

"The daughter and the gardener loved each other so much that they decided to run away together into the world outside the garden. They hid in the gardens—all night, the delicate lady hid in a spidery, dark shed. But the cruel father discovered their secret and searched the garden at dawn. The only way out was over the lake, across a narrow bridge. When the lovers came out of hiding and made to leave the garden, there on the bridge stood the cruel father, whip in hand, ready to kill the poor young gardener. When the lovers saw that it was impossible to escape, they jumped off the bridge, thinking to drown together in the lake."

Then Liu would come bursting into his story and exclaim, "But the gods smiled on them and turned them into bluebirds, and they flew away to lasting happiness!"

Then Wa Fan said, "You know my story already," and Liu blushed and covered her mouth with her fingers and trotted to the door on her wooden heels and clattered back to her father's house.

You see Liu loved Wa Fan the potter, and Wa Fan loved her. But they could no more hope to be married than a fish can hope to fly.

One day, cruel Ho Pa said to his daughter, "You may thank me, Liu. Prepare yourself. Whiten your face and redden your lips and dress your hair with flowers. For I have found you a husband."

Liu bowed low to her father. "I will indeed thank you, father, if the husband you have chosen is Wa Fan, your apprentice. He is a fine man."

"Who?" cried Ho Pa. "Ha! Do you suppose I would marry a daughter of mine to a worthless apprentice? No! You shall marry Chu Fat, the merchant, whose wealth is as huge as his belly and whose business sense is as quick as

158

his temper and whose reputation is almost as old as he. He shall sell my pottery, and together we shall grow richer than the Emperor himself. You shall marry tomorrow. Speak no more of Wa Fan."

Liu said nothing. In old China, during the Ch'ing dynasty and in the days of the Manchu Emperor Ch'ien Lung, a daughter's words were worth less than dead leaves blowing down a street. But the birds of sadness pecked at her heart.

In those days, Ho Pa rarely went to his pottery, for he had Wa Fan to do all his work and Wa Fan's china was finer than anything Ho Pa could ever make with his own hands. Now he went straight there, and walked up and down the racks, pretending to examine the plates and vases and bowls.

"Tell me, Wa Fan, what do you think of my daughter?" he asked casually. He saw the apprentice's hand tremble as he painted the leaves onto a blue willow tree.

"She is the pattern of all beauty, master; a creation more perfect than any vase shaped by hand, any words written by poets, any music sung by minstrels."

"And what would you say if I told you you could marry her?"

Wa Fan dropped his paintbrush altogether and leaped up from his stool. "I would say that you are the best of men and that I am the happiest!"

Then Ho Pa held his sides and laughed till the tears ran down his fat cheeks. "Hear this, you shineless pebble on a dusty road: my daughter will be married tomorrow to Chu Fat, the merchant, and I shall stop your wages for daring to rest your eyes upon my daughter! Ha! ha! ha! What do you say to that?"

Wa Fan said nothing. For in old China, during the Ch'ing dynasty and in the days of the Manchu Emperor Ch'ien Lung, the words of an apprentice were worth less than the ants in a spadeful of earth. But inwardly the dogs of sadness chewed on his heart.

"Some token of respect—some present for the happy pair —would be acceptable," said Ho Pa, sweeping out of the door.

Wa Fan went to the window and looked out at the splendid gardens which surrounded Ho Pa's still more splendid house. The orange blossom was tearful with rain. The willow tree by the lake slumped with rounded shoulders. The lake glimmered through the reeds like teardrops on the lashes of a great sad eye. Wa Fan looked for a long time at the little bridge hunched over the lake. Then he fetched a plain, undecorated plate of finest pottery and glazed it white as milk, and then began to paint, in a glaze as blue as purple, one last Willow-Pattern story.

It was work more perfect than any Wa Fan had ever done before.

He baked the plate in the kiln and the figures and flowers stood out so brightly that they seemed to move across the little bridge beside the ornamental lake and the painted pagodas. In them the fate of Wa Fan was fastened. He could not turn back now.

On the morning of the wedding, Wa Fan went to the market and bought strawberries, and heaped them on the plate and dredged them with sugar, and took them to the door of the great house where his master lived. Bowing very low to the doorkeeper, he said, "Please set this miserable and worthless present before the bride and groom, and say that it is a token of respect from the insignificant Wa Fan, apprentice."

The contracts had been signed. Liu sat at table beside the gross and wheezing Chu Fat—like a golden carp beside a whale. The tasseled rods and flowered combs fastening her hair trembled, and her eyes were fixed on her lap. Her father sat at the head of the table, drinking toasts to himself and his ancestors in cups of rice wine, and laughing immoderately.

The doorkeeper brought in a plate of strawberries and set it down between the bride and groom. "A token of respect

from the insignificant Wa Fan, apprentice." Liu started a
little, and her father let out a roar of laughter big enough to
fill a ship's sail. The bridegroom plunged a fat hand in
among the strawberries and crammed twenty into his food-
clogged mouth.

Liu rested her gaze on the blue rim of the plate. She had
no eyes for the strawberries. She loved Wa Fan, and so she
loved to look at his beautiful craftsmanship. She smiled
sadly to see the picture emerge from beneath the
strawberries as her betrothed crammed the fruit into his
face.

No one saw her shoulders stiffen, her eyes grow wide, or her fingers crumple the edge of the tablecloth. For during the Ch'ing dynasty, in the days of the Manchu Emperor Ch'ien Lung, a woman learned to be silent and unnoticeable in the eyes of men. She took one strawberry from the plate. And then another.

She was not mistaken. Her own face looked up at her from the blue and white garden of the Willow Pattern. She it was, who stood on the bridge hand in hand with the poor gardener.

Another strawberry.

And there was her father—there was Ho Pa in every shape and feature, standing on the bridge. There was his angry scowl, his vain heap of hair, his big fist grasping the whip, his twisted mouth swearing vengeance.

Another strawberry and oh!

Who was it who stood hand in hand with her on the legendary bridge but Wa Fan, the apprentice, dressed in gardener's clothes but quite unmistakable to the eyes of one who loved him. A perfect self-portrait.

The plate was a message. The plate was a letter, a plea, a proposal. The plate said, "Run away with me, Liu, for I love you as the gardener loved the rich merchant's daughter in the Willow-Pattern story."

Liu's lips parted and she said, so silently that only her ancestors heard her, "Yes, yes, Wa Fan. I will come."

"Pass those strawberries to me, daughter, or have you no respect for your father?"

Liu's heart fluttered between her ribs like a bird caught in a trap. The faces on the plate were showing clearly now. Wa Fan's plan was laid bare. It was there for everyone to see. Would Wa Fan not pay for his daring with life itself?

"Daughter! Bring me the plate!"

She could not disobey. She carried the plate to her father and he ate the remaining strawberries. Only a snow of sugar still rested on the blue and white shining garden of the Willow Pattern.

Ho Pa picked it up and examined it. "I see Wa Fan has done his finest work for my daughter's wedding gift."

But though he looked at the cruel and raging face of the man on the bridge, he did not recognize himself. For Ho Pa was vain and he thought himself handsome. He did not recognize the face of the girl on the bridge, for he had never cared enough to look closely into her face. And he did not recognize the face of his apprentice, for he had never looked upon Wa Fan as a man, only as a pair of hands which earned him money: a tool, an object, a thing. He turned to his daughter and said, "Fetch more strawberries. The plate is empty."

He handed it into her hands—Wa Fan's priceless wedding gift into her hands. He sent her from the room when all she had lacked was an excuse to leave the room.

Along the corridor she hurried, holding the plate to her breast—out into the garden where the sun shone smilingly, past the chrysanthemums, the painted pagoda, and along the lake shore to the little bridge. There, hidden among the tresses of the willow tree, she found Wa Fan, his long pigtail held anxiously between his nervous fingers.

"You came," he said.

"I came," she said.

"You have left behind everything for me," he said.

"I have left behind nothing, she said, "for look, I have the present you sent me and that is all in the world that I prize. I will never part with it."

Then they crossed over the hunched little bridge, hand in hand, and into the world beyond.

They went to the harbor, and there they found a Portuguese merchant ship making ready to sail.

"Carry us to your faraway land in the West," said Wa Fan to the Portuguese captain.

The captain—a swarthy man, fearful to Chinese eyes with his coarse-bearded jaw and big moist eyes—looked at the ragged Wa Fan and at Liu in her wedding dress. He plucked at his lip. He looked in vain for their luggage.

"And how will you pay me, Chinaman?"

"With hard work and thanks," said Wa Fan.

"Oh many, many thanks," said Liu.

But the sea captain's heart was as cold and sharp-pointed as the anchor of his ship. It lay like a moneybag within his chest and its purse-strings were pulled tight. "I vouch some father will pay me well for the return of his daughter," he said, twirling his dark mustache. "Some bridegroom will pay me well for the return of his bride."

"No, no!" cried Liu, covering her face.

"No, no!" cried Wa Fan, shielding her with his arm. And the sea gaped, and the waves gasped, the topsail shook in the wind.

Then the captain saw the plate which Liu held to her breast. His eyes gleamed and his hands could not help but reach for it. "Did you say you had no fare? This is Willow-Pattern china from the pottery of Ho Pa and the finest piece I ever saw. This will pay your fare!"

He snatched at the plate, he fumbled, and the delicate porcelain fell between ship and dockside. It floated on the water like a lily.

Into the water leaped Wa Fan and seized the plate and held it high over his head, and the sea captain snatched it—more precious to him than a child—from its watery destruction.

"Wait!" said Wa Fan struggling ashore. "The plate does not belong to me!"

The captain turned, scowling. "What's that? Is it stolen?"

"No, indeed! But it is the property of this lady, and only

she may give it away!"

Liu looked long at the beautiful plate dripping between the sea captain's hands. At last she said, "What is china compared with the fate of two hearts? What is a plate compared with the face of my Wa Fan! What is a thing made with hands, compared with the hands which made it?"

So Wa Fan and Liu set sail across a tangle of foam, toward the shores of distant Europe. Their souls were so filled with invisible joy as to fly like two birds above the ship, whiter than the flapping sail.

Meanwhile, the sea captain kept below decks and gloated over a thing molded from clay and painted with the colors of crushed flowers. He thought the plate a rich addition to his cargo. But there are those who believe he had aboard his ship a far greater treasure.

"Oh Brian!" said the girl.

"Oh Traycie!" said the boy.

"Oh buy it for me, Brian!"

"Don't be daft. It must be worth hundreds."

"Not necessarily," said M. C. C., and his eyes were as deep and dark as the South China seas but quite empty of sharks. "Value doesn't always show itself in the price."

Brian groped a handful of coins out of his jeans, and Ailsa wrapped the plate in tissue paper. She meant to scratch off any disappointing, telltale English pottery mark on the back, but there wasn't one. There was only a long, dangling, Chinese cipher shaped like a chain of paper lanterns.

"Where's the sweet little book?" wondered Traycie, searching about in the region of the *chaise longue.*

"What book's that?" said M. C. C., resting his hand in the pocket of his green corduroy jacket.

A PROPOSALE

DAISY ASHFORD

The Young Visiters, or, Mr. Salteenas Plan, published in 1919,
was the work of Daisy Ashford, aged nine. My own copy, quite an
old one, is child-sized with a sepia photograph of Daisy in the front.
She is rosy faced and wears a cheeky grin and a sailor's collar. This
extract retains Daisy's original spelling which is all part of the fun.
I think it is one of the most hilarious books ever written.

NEXT MORNING while imbibing his morning tea beneath his pink silken quilt Bernard decided he must marry Ethel with no more delay. I love the girl he said to himself and she must be mine but I somehow feel I can not propose in London it would not be seemly in the city of London. We must go for a day in the country and when surrounded by the gay twittering of the birds and the smell of the cows I will lay my suit at her feet and he waved his arm wildly at the gay thought. Then he sprang from bed and gave a rat tat at Ethel's door.

Are you up my dear he called.

Well not quite said Ethel hastily jumping from her downy nest.

Be quick cried Bernard I have a plan to spend a day near Windsor Castle and we will take our lunch and spend a happy day.

Oh Hurrah shouted Ethel I shall soon be ready as I had my bath last night so wont wash very much now.

No dont said Bernard and added in a rarther fervent tone through the chink of the door you are fresher than the rose my dear no soap could make you fairer.

Then he dashed off very embarrassed to dress. Ethel blushed and felt a bit excited as she heard the words and she put on a new white muslin dress in a fit of high spirits. She looked very beautifull with some red roses in her hat and the dainty red ruge in her cheeks looked quite the thing. Bernard heaved a sigh and his eyes flashed as he beheld her and Ethel thorght to herself what a fine type of manhood he reprisented with his nice thin legs in pale broun trousers and well fitting spats and a red rose in his button hole and rarther a sporting cap which gave him a great air with its quaint check and little flaps to pull down if necesarry. Off they started the envy of all the waiters.

They arrived at Windsor very hot from the jorney and Bernard at once hired a boat to row his beloved up the river. Ethel could not row but she much enjoyed seeing the tough sunburnt arms of Bernard tugging at the oars as she lay among the rich cushons of the dainty boat. She had a rarther lazy nature but Bernard did not know of this. However he soon got dog tired and sugested lunch by the mossy bank.

Oh yes said Ethel quickly opening the sparkling champaigne.

Dont spill any cried Bernard as he carved some chicken.

They eat and drank deeply of the charming viands ending up with merangs and choclates.

Let us now bask under the spreading trees said Bernard in a passiunate tone.

Oh yes lets said Ethel and she opened her dainty parasole and sank down upon the long green grass. She closed her eyes but she was far from asleep. Bernard sat beside her in profound silence gazing at her pink face and long wavy eye lashes. He puffed at his pipe for some moments while the larks gaily caroled in the blue sky. Then he edged a trifle closer to Ethels form.

Ethel he murmered in a trembly voice.

Oh what is it said Ethel hastily sitting up.

Words fail me ejaculated Bernard horsly my passion for you is intense he added fervently. It has grown day and night since I first beheld you.

Oh said Ethel in supprise I am not prepared for this and she lent back against the trunk of the tree.

Bernard placed one arm tightly round her. When will you marry me Ethel he uttered you must be my wife it has come to that I love you so intensly that if you say no I shall perforce dash my body to the brink of yon muddy river he panted wildly.

Oh dont do that implored Ethel breathing rarther hard.

Then say you love me he cried.

Oh Bernard she sighed fervently I certinly love you madly you are to me like a Heathen god she cried looking at his manly form and handsome flashing face I will indeed marry you.

How soon gasped Bernard gazing at her intensly.

As soon as possible said Ethel gently closing her eyes.

My Darling whispered Bernard and he seiezed her in his arms we will be marrid next week.

Oh Bernard muttered Ethel this is so sudden.

No no cried Bernard and taking the bull by both horns he kissed her violently on her dainty face. My bride to be he murmered several times.

Ethel trembled with joy as she heard the mistick words.

Oh Bernard she said little did I ever dream of such as this and she suddenly fainted into his out stretched arms.

Oh I say gasped Bernard and laying the dainty burden on the grass he dashed to the waters edge and got a cup full of the fragrant river to pour on his true loves pallid brow.

She soon came to and looked up with a sickly smile Take me back to the Gaierty hotel she whispered faintly.

With plesure my darling said Bernard I will just pack up our viands ere I unloose the boat.

Ethel felt better after a few drops of champagne and began to tidy her hair while Bernard packed the remains of the food. Then arm in arm they tottered to the boat.

I trust you have not got an illness my darling murmered Bernard as he helped her in.

Oh no I am very strong said Ethel I fainted from joy she added to explain matters.

Oh I see said Bernard handing her a cushon well some people do he added kindly and so saying they rowed down the dark stream now flowing silently beneath a golden moon. All was silent as the lovers glided home with joy in their hearts and radiunce on their faces only the sound of the mystearious water lapping against the frail vessel broke the monotony of the night.

So I will end my chapter.

I WAS ADORED ONCE, TOO

JAN MARK

"IN THE BEGINNING Birkett created the heaven and the earth," said Birkett. "And the earth was without form, and void; and darkness was upon the face of the deep."

"Geddonwithit, Birk," shouted voices in the darkness, up on the stage and down in the auditorium. Someone fell over a chair.

Working blind, he clipped off a length of wire and threaded it into the fuse.

"And the Spirit of Birkett moved upon the face of the waters . . ." He snapped the fuse into its socket and put his hand on the master switch. ". . . And Birkett said, Let there be light: and there was light."

At once, all the lights; white light from the floats and the battens, rose-pink light and amber from the floods, and eight suns hanging in the void beyond the stage, four on each side of the hall.

"Not bad, not bad," said Cosgrove, who was standing a few feet away and had heard everything that he said. "Now let's see you make a man."

171

Birkett leaned over the rail of his crow's nest by the switchboard and looked round the edge of the curtain. Way below the white giants a red dwarf was approaching the footlights, surrounded by a nebula: Mr. Anderson, head of English, with his everlasting cigarette and his checkered cheese-cutter pulled well down over his eyes to protect them from the glare.

What could they call him but Andy Capp? They called him Andy Capp.

Andy Capp came up to the edge of the stage and leaned across the floats, shielding himself from them by cupping his hands under his eyes and peering through the mask of black shadow like a seedy bandit.

"When Birkett has finished trying to blow his hand off, perhaps we can get on with the rehearsal?"

Birkett drew back from the edge of his cast-iron cradle and set his hands to the dimmer switches. His lighting plot was tacked up above them, secretively recorded in his own shorthand:

P36 l. 15 exit M. DI down 5 D2 down 10 simul.
l. 20 D2 down 0 D3/4 down 5 change spots to dim
here 1/2/3/4.

The light came and went at his command. He was far less likely to blow off his hand than was Andy Capp himself. When Andy Capp came up on stage and stood at the foot of Birkett's vertical iron ladder, Birkett wanted nothing so much as to put his foot on Andy Capp's head and screw it down into the floor, as the English teacher screwed down his own boot on his cigarette butts.

Andy Capp knew this as well as Birkett did, and stayed on the other side of the footlights, within spitting distance of Birkett but safe; because Andy Capp was Sir and Birkett was in 5b, good for fiddling with the lights and little else.

Fiddling was the right word. Birkett played on his dimmers with the love and skill of a virtuoso violinist, making night and day, the greater light and the lesser, with the tenderest touch of his long and flexible fingers. The woodwork master, now Stage Manager, was well aware of this, which was why he had given Birkett the lighting plot instead of doing it himself. As far as Andy Capp was concerned, Birkett was marooned on top of his ladder because he could do less damage there than he could on-stage, mangling Shakespeare.

And he could mend a fuse in the dark.

Birkett consulted the plot and without looking, placed his unerring hands on the dimmers. His eye was on the stage where Cosgrove, a pillow stuffed under his sweater, was reeling from side to side, supposedly drunk. Cosgrove, when genuinely drunk, was nothing like this, but after the effects had worn off he never could remember what it had been like. Cosgrove's mates had sworn to have him tanked up on the night so as to get an authentic performance out of him.

"Listen, Cosgrove," said Andy Capp. Birkett's hands froze on the dimmers. "This is *Twelfth Night*, not Saturday night at the Bricklayer's Arms. Sir Toby Belch is supposed to be tipsy in this scene, not paralytic."

Cosgrove snapped upright and Howell, who was playing Sir Andrew Aguecheek, was knocked flying by the cushion. He went spinning across the stage, stiff-legged, like dividers across a map.

"Aguecheek," said Andy Capp "is a foolish knight, not a berserk ballerina. Keep your twinkle toes on the ground. Get on with it, rabble." His eyes slid upward and sideways. Birkett knew that Andy Capp had something offensive ready to say to him as well, but there was no occasion to say it. Sir Toby and Sir Andrew faced each other; Sir Andrew's mouth opened and the dimmers began to move.

"Before me, she's a good wench," said Sir Andrew.

"She's a beagle, true-bred, and one that adores me; what o' that?"

Sir Andrew raised his eyebrows. "I was adored once, too."

"Howell! Don't sound so bloody chatty," Andy Capp bellowed from the darkness. "That's one of your better lines. Make something of it. Like this." He minced about beyond the footlights, now in focus, now out. "*I* was adored once *too*."

"Oh, ducky," murmured Cosgrove, out of the corner of his mouth.

"Get a laugh there," said Andy Capp. "It's the last one you'll get in this scene. And Birkett, keep your hot little hands off those dimmers. Are you trying to black us out?" Birkett let his hands drop. He had planned to make the light turn cold on that line, dimming out the amber and the rose, leaving only the white and blue battens. He had not bargained for a laugh; it didn't strike him as funny. There was a character in the play known as the Clown, but he was a wise guy, a professional fool. Aguecheek was the real fool.

"*I* was adored once *too*," said Howell, flimsy-wristed, gyrating on pleated ankles. He had tucked his trousers into his socks to make himself feel Elizabethan. There was an immediate laugh from the resting actors, out of sight in the dark hall.

174

"Again!" cried Andy Capp.

"*I* was adored once, *too.*"

There were two more scenes before the end of the act. On the stage below the players strutted, and at the switchboard above Birkett lightened their darkness and darkened their days. He felt as remote as God, operating the firmament; whatever was going on down there had nothing to do with him. The pain and the pleasure were outside his influence and he felt them only in terms of the colored filters required to light each scene: blue and green for sorrow, pink and gold for joy, so that when he looked at the brilliant aquarium that was the stage he saw chaos. People hid behind hedges, assumed false names, slipped into disguises and climbed out of them. Lesley Pascoe, smooth and slender, golden girl of the High School, was cast as Viola, identical twin to Sebastian, and Sebastian was played by swarthy Noddy Newton who was so covered with thick black hair that when he tried on his costume it sprouted through the legs of his tights like winter wheat after a wet autumn.

All the female roles were being played by girls borrowed from the High School. As well as the three principals a number of friends turned up at each rehearsal to understudy or provide moral support in case anyone got jumped on in a dark cloakroom. Birkett knew none of them. They were the girls who went round with the boys who were down there on the stage; none of them people who would go round with Birkett.

It was nothing to do with him. He saw it and heard it and was out of it; even so, the words stayed in his mind, like dust caught in a net curtain. In the same way, and without wanting to, he had memorized the Bible. For years he had been a regular worshiper, with his parents, at the green tin chapel behind the bus station. One Sunday he had suddenly realized that he was no longer worshiping and after a month or two he stopped going there, but the damage was done already. It was widely believed that

Birkett had sold his soul to the chapel and was stricken, unable to enjoy himself, drink beer or think about women. People half expected him to turn up on the doorstep with leaflets, at inconvenient moments.

He looked down from the switchboard, one of them, but not one with them.

"To the gates of Tartar, thou most excellent devil of wit!" Sir Toby shouted. He strode offstage and made a mock run up the ladder, repelled suddenly by the impact of his cushion against the rungs.

"And I'll make one too," said Sir Andrew Aguecheek, with total irrelevance, as it seemed to Birkett. He wandered off in the other direction. Cosgrove's spotty brother who was prompter and Assistant Stage Manager, swung on the knotted rope that dangled beside his chair. The curtains closed on Birkett's sunlit stage and Act Two was over. Cosgrove poked the cushion out of his sweater and looked up at Birkett.

"Don't you get struck by lightning for blasphemy?"

"Blasphemy?"

"Smitten with a plague of frogs?"

"Blasphemy?"

"Taking credit for the Universe," said Cosgrove, but because Birkett had nothing laughable to say he lost interest and slid between the curtains, sylph-slim without his stomach which he left onstage. He disappeared into the dark hall, followed by Howell.

"House lights!" Andy Capp was bawling. "House lights, Birkett wake up for God's sake Birkett wake up Birkett . . ."

Howell put his head between the curtains again. "Fiat lux, laddie. Fiat lux." Howell knew Latin. Birkett didn't. The house lights were not his concern anyway; the switches were at the back of the hall, next to the wall bars. Finally someone remembered this and the lights were put on. Andy Capp's monotonous yelling subsided and cheerful conversation swelled up to fill the gap where it had been. Cups rattled. The girls who were not onstage had made themselves responsible for serving drinks (although no one had dared ask them to) which they prepared in the Sixth Form Common Room and brought to the hall on trays. The spotty brother and other backstage personnel went through the curtains for coffee and fodder. Birkett stayed at the switchboard, setting up his lights for the next act. It was the same scene, but a different time of day:

Olivia's Garden. Full battens white 1/2 dim 0 blue 3.
Amber floods full floats. 1/2/3/4 spots up full 5/6 down 8.

He made morning.

Number six dimmer was grating in its runner. Knowing that he had a quarter of an hour before Andy Capp drove the cast back to work Birkett took out a screwdriver and began to remove the casing. He first put up the master switch and worked in darkness, only his careful hands illuminated by the meager glow from a badly shuttered window in the changing room behind him. In the corner of his eye he saw a narrow light spread across the stage and ebb again as someone opened the curtains and slipped through. Finished with the dimmer he replaced the casing and threw the masterswitch. There came an angry squeak from the foot of the ladder.

"Ow. Now you've made me spill it."

One of the girls was standing there, clasping a thick china cup of slopped coffee. Birkett leaned over the rail.

"Was that my fault?"

"You made me jump, putting all the lights on like that." She squinted up at him. He looked at the coffee cup.

"You haven't lost much. There's plenty left."

"It isn't mine."

"There's no one else here," said Birkett.

"You're here."

"Is it for me?" Nobody had brought him coffee before. There was no reason why he should not join the others in the hall, but apart from wanting a drink there was no

177

reason why he should. He preferred to do without the drink.

"I suppose it must be," she said. "I was handing it out and Tony Cosgrove said, 'Don't forget God, back there,' so I brought it through. Do they call you God?"

"They call me Birk," said Birkett.

"Well, do you want the coffee or don't you, Birk?" said the girl. "I'm not going to call you that," she said crossly. "What's your real name?"

"Reuben," said Birkett, reluctantly. The Twelve Tribes of Israel were highly thought of at the tin chapel. He disliked admitting to Reuben, but he had no second name. It could have been worse. It could have been Zebulun. Or Gad.

"I'm Juliet." She offered him the coffee, but when he made no move to take it she withdrew her hand. "Call me Julie. Can I come up?"

"Juliet will do." It didn't occur to him that one could suffer as much from Juliet as from Reuben. "You can come up if you like."

She stood on tiptoe and placed the cup on the floor of the cradle. It was difficult for her to stand more on tiptoe than she did already: her wedge heels were very high.

"You'd better take your shoes off," he advised. She looked suspicious, as if he had made an improper suggestion and her friends had warned her about people like him, but she came up the ladder, her lumpy heels going glamp glamp glamp as they struck the iron rungs.

"You are a bit like God, so high up," she said, leaning against the rail. Birkett, pressed for space, had to turn round with extreme care in case she thought he was making advances.

"Turn the lights off again," she said.

Now who's making advances! he wondered, as the darkness crashed down.

"It's snug up here."

"About as snug as an oil rig." Now that it was entirely dark he was aware of the draft from the changing room window and the smell of old lunches that never quite died because the stage had once been used as a canteen, before the new one was built. The hot lights seemed to revive it. He pulled the switch again and Juliet stood blinking beside him.

"Birkett, stop b-ing about with those lights," shouted Andy Capp, mindful that there were ladies present.

"Aren't you going to drink your coffee?" said Juliet. Birkett stepped forward to pick up the cup and managed to kick it over the edge of the cradle. It didn't break, but a grayer stain spread over the gray stage cloth.

"I'm always doing things like that," he said.

"I was beginning to think you never did anything," said Juliet, and went glamping down the ladder again. He put his head under the lower rail and watched her go.

"Are you in the play?" he said. "I've never seen you on-stage."

"I'm a servant. Page sixty, Act Three. Scene Four, don't blink or you'll miss me." He didn't say that he thought she was wasted as a servant. "I'm understudying Maria, too."

179

"That's the maid, isn't it?"

"It's the best part," she said, quickly.

"I thought Lesley Pascoe . . ."

"Oh, Viola. That's nothing much. Maria's got the best lines of all the women. And she's funny," said Juliet. She went toward the curtains with the empty cup. "It's the best part . . . but you wouldn't know," she said, and vanished.

She was right. He didn't know.

That night he read the play right through for the first time, and he was surprised to discover how much of it he knew already. He agreed that Maria was the best of the women's parts, but he doubted that Juliet would make much of a showing in it. Maria was a stinger; little, quick-witted, malicious. He thought of Juliet's large hopeful face and pile-driver legs.

On Thursday evening, when they stopped for a break, there was Juliet coming up the ladder glamp glamp glamp with two cups of coffee and a KitKat. His half of the KitKat played merry hell with his demon back tooth, but he suffered in silence, showing her how the dimmers worked and explaining the runic mysteries of his lighting plot.

"Do you manage all this by yourself? I wouldn't have thought you'd have enough hands."

He spread his fingers across the board and moved all eight dimmers at once.

"Like a pianist," Juliet said. "Stretching octaves. What about if you need to turn something else on, at the same time?"

"I use my nose. No. I *do*. In the mad scene where Malvolio thinks he's in the nuthouse: I turn off this switch here with my nose. Like this."

"Well, it's long enough." Juliet didn't seem to think that it was a very nice accomplishment. "You need Tony Cosgrove up here. He's all hands."

"He'd be no good," said Birkett. "He'd be talking all the

time. You have to pay attention."

"There's no one to talk to."

"There would be if Cosgrove was here."

At the end of the break Juliet remained at the top of the ladder.

"You don't mind if I stay?"

"Of course not." He should have said Oh please, do. In fact, he did mind. The cradle was built to take at most two people, both working. There was no room for ballast. Birkett was used to availing himself of the whole area and the need to tread carefully spoiled his concentration. For the first time he missed a lighting cue and was rewarded by a blast of scorching scorn from Andy Capp, who happened to notice, for once. The sympathetic touch of Juliet's hand on his arm was no reward, and no consolation, either.

Cosgrove, bleary and becushioned, leered at him, one finger laid to the side of his nose.

"Nudge, nudge, wink, wink," said Cosgrove, when he came offstage at the end of the scene and Birkett was embarrassed in the dark; but at the same time mildly gratified that Cosgrove imagined him to be having his evil way—as Cosgrove certainly would have been, in his place.

At the next rehearsal Juliet was up there before him.

"Aren't you on in this scene?"

"Fancy you noticing."

"I read the play." He had read it again since last week. He was beginning to admire the way it was put together; two quite different stories spliced like cords, ending in a neat knot, but he didn't find it very funny and parts of it struck him as miserably cruel. He had always regarded Shakespeare as an effete twit who couldn't write a straight sentence to save his life, but he was beginning to see that Shakespeare might have got along very well with Andy Capp.

"Another bride, another groom, another sunny huhunnymoon," sang Cosgrove at the foot of the ladder. "Make with the sunshine, Birk."

Juliet was picking her way through the lighting plot.

"I don't expect anyone but us understands this," she said happily, building an intimate secret where there was neither secret nor intimacy. "I'm not onstage until here, look. I can run round the back, just before."

And she did: and as soon as her little part was done she ran back again. Birkett did not hear her coming up the ladder. She had taken her shoes off.

"Don't you want to go for coffee?" said Birkett, when the break came.

"I asked Lesley to bring us some." He guessed why she had asked Lesley when Lesley came through the curtains with a sulky shove, carrying a cup in either hand.

"Too busy to fetch your own?"

Juliet smiled a little, and then laughed, because the light was too dim for the smile to show. Birkett waited until Lesley had gone before sitting down to drink his coffee.

"It's a good thing we aren't fat," said Juliet.

"Eh?"

"There's not much room up here."

"We could always sit on the stage." He stood up to consult the plot.

"Hey, Roo." He supposed that it was short for Reuben.

"Yes?"

"I'm glad I'm not Viola."

"You're even less like Noddy than Lesley is."

"That's not what I meant. She's onstage, all through the play."

"Not all the time."

"No, but on-off-on-off. It's the same with Maria. Suzanne's playing Maria. Do you know Suzanne? She's all sweaty by the end of the evening, from rushing about."

"Dodging Cosgrove?"

"And that. I used to wish she'd be ill for a bit so that I'd get a chance at Maria; tonsillitis or something. She's got terrible tonsils, all her family have. When she turns her head you can see great lumps in her neck—just here." She put her cool hand on his throat.

"I've had mine out," said Birkett.

"I don't wish that anymore."

"Wish what?"

"That Suzanne would get tonsillitis. I'd sooner be here than onstage."

"Well, I wouldn't wish anyone had tonsillitis," said Birkett. "Except Andy Capp, maybe. It might shut him up."

"Roo, why do you call him Andy Capp?"

"Oh God, look at him," said Birkett. "All he needs is a pigeon on his head."

"What's his wife like? Florrie?"

"More like the Statue of Liberty. No, really. He hardly

183

comes up to her chin."

"Have they got any children?"

"Three."

"I like children," said Juliet. "I'd like a lot of children."

There was only one week left before opening night. In front of the curtain the stage had been extended by building it up with prefabricated blocks. Andy Capp called it the apron.

When the third act ended, Howell climbed over the apron and came through the curtains with the coffee. Juliet arranged for it to be delivered by a different person each time, and Birkett no longer wondered why.

"Working overtime, Birk?" said Howell. He stood on the bottom rung of the ladder and rested his chin on the top, level with their feet.

"Push off, Face-ache," said Birkett.

"Aguecheek—Agueface—Face-ache; good thinking, Batman," said Howell, sinking from sight. He reappeared a moment later, meandering across the stage in his Aguecheek walk, knees together, toes apart.

"You missed your cue again, in Scene Four," said Howell. "Do you know what Andy Capp said? 'Bloody Birkett busy with his skirt.'"

"He never said that." Beside him Juliet gave a little gasp, intending to sound outraged; only sounding pleased.

"It was said though," said Howell. "Your Birk-type secret is out, Birk." He sprang backward between the curtains. Nemesis got him. Someone had removed the block in the middle of the apron, and Birkett heard the crunch as he hit the floor.

"He's broken his leg; in two places. Should have been his neck," said Andy Capp. "He's in traction. Silly b—." There were ladies present.

"What about my bruvver?" said Cosgrove. "He's been prompter ever since we started. He knows the whole thing right through."

184

"He couldn't play Aguecheek."

"He could probably play Viola if you twisted his arm."

"God forbid," said Andy Capp. "Anyway, we're not having him onstage. Remember the carol concert?"

"Someone else knows it by heart," said Cosgrove. He silently indicated the switchboard with his thumb. "He remembers everything. He knows half the Bible for a start."

"Birkett? He can't put one foot in front of the other without falling over."

"Who'd notice? He's a dead ringer for Aguecheek," said Cosgrove. "You wouldn't even have to make him up."

"Birkett! Get down here," Andy Capp shouted. "If you can spare the time," he added, for the benefit of the cast. Birkett climbed down the ladder and approached the group in the middle of the stage.

"Good of you to drop in," said Andy Capp. "I'm sure you've got more interesting things to do. Cosgrove here says you're a quick study."

"A what?"

"A quick study, har har," said Andy Capp. "He says you learn things easily."

"Not me," said Birkett.

"He thinks you know the whole play."

"Not me."

"Come off it," said Cosgrove. "You've been sitting up there watching us for the past six months. You must know it."

Birkett guessed what they were after.

"Not me."

"Not I," said Andy Capp.

Cosgrove put on his cushion and his Sir Toby voice and said sharply, "Did she see thee the while, old boy? Tell me that."

"As plain as I see you now," said Birkett, without thinking.

"Art thou good at these kick-shaws, knight?"

"As any man in Illyria, whatsoever he be, under the

185

degree of my betters; and yet I will not compare with an old man," said Birkett.

"She's a beagle, true-bred, and one that adores me; what o' that?"

"*I was adored once too.*"

"Beat that," said Cosgrove.

Andy Capp thrust a book into Birkett's hands. "There you are, Aguecheek. Get on with it."

"But I don't understand it all."

"Then you'll have a lot in common with the audience," said Andy Capp. "You have a week. Get on with it."

"Who'll do the lights?" said Birkett. "I'm the only one who knows the plot."

"Damn the lights. What's the good of lights if we have no play?" said Andy Capp. "Leave 'em all switched on. Come on, rabble. Act One, Scene Three."

The rehearsal got under way. Birkett held the book in his hands and never looked at it once. When it was his turn to speak he spoke, helplessly, the very words that Howell had spoken, and in the very tone that Howell had spoken them.

"Proper polly parrot, aren't you?" muttered Cosgrove, when he stumbled on his lines and Birkett prompted him, still without looking at the book. "You taking English 'A' level, next year?"

"You're joking."

"Do it. You'll have a walkover."

At the end of the scene Birkett ran from the stage and made for the ladder, hoping that he would have time to get up there and adjust the lights before he was wanted, but as he put his hands to the rungs the floods came on and the dimmers went up. Juliet looked over the railing.

"Don't worry about me, Roo. I can manage."

He hadn't been worrying about her. He had forgotten that she was there.

"I told you I could understand it."

"Better leave it," said Birkett, furious at finding his true place usurped. "I've made alterations—you won't be able to follow them."

"I know your writing," said Juliet, comfortably. "Go back onstage. You're doing ever so well. I didn't know you were so good."

"I'm not," he growled, and thought it was true. He was a proper polly parrot.

"You, Birkett, are a double-dyed creep," said Andy Capp, leaning across the apron. "Is this the case that dropped a thousand bricks? Is this the celebrated numb-skull who has forgotten to hand in his homework six weeks out of nine? Well, we've found you out now, you twister."

"Polly parrot," said Birkett, under his breath.

"Get on with it, rabble."

They got on with it, and Juliet got on with the lights. Birkett knew to the second when a change was due, and to the second the changes were made. He made a note to dim number two spot when he had the chance. It shone straight in his eye every time he faced right.

"Excellent," Sir Toby roared in his ear. "I smell a device."

"I have't in my nose too," said Birkett, in a reedy nasal whine, out-Howelling Howell. A happy laugh surged out of the darkness.

Sir Toby roared longer and louder, piqued that Birkett was getting bigger laughs than he was.

"My purpose is indeed a horse of that color," said

Maria, arching her long neck like a thoroughbred. Birkett could see no sign of swollen tonsils.

"And your horse would now make him an ass," he said, and was half drowned by another high tide of laughter. They were laughing at him, not with him, but he supposed that that was what he was there for.

Maria spoke again and went out, blowing kisses to Sir Toby.

"Good night, Penthesilia," said Sir Toby.

"Before me, she's a good wench," said Birkett.

"She's a beagle, true-bred, and one that adores me; what o' that?"

"*I* was adored once *too*." The laughter exploded all round him as he stood there, a dead ringer for Sir Andrew Aguecheek; lank yellow hair drooping over his white face, round eyes staring, long arms dangling. What a thought; Birkett; adored; har har, as Andy Capp would say.

Suddenly the lights turned blue, stuttered, went dim, became bright again, went out entirely and then came on in a frightful blaze, all eight suns burning him alive.

"What the hell is going on?" demanded Andy Capp, vaulting onto the apron like a galvanized leprechaun and hurling his copy of the play across the stage. "Who did that?"

Birkett turned to the switchboard in a rage.

"You silly cow! Leave it alone. I altered that bit. I said you wouldn't understand it."

"Who's up there? Who is it? Come down here, now," said Andy Capp, more terrible in a whisper than he ever was at full volume.

Juliet came down the ladder glamp glamp glamp on her club heels and stumbled toward them. Her face was a brighter pink than any floodlight could have made it, and her eyes were enormous with tears.

"I thought . . ."

"Thought?" Andy Capp was incredulous. "Who asked you to think? Who asked you to touch the switchboard? It's a skilled job, not a game for silly little girls."

Juliet moved toward Birkett. Birkett moved away.

"I told you," he said.

"I thought I knew it," said Juliet. She bent her head and the tears fell to the floor. They made grayer spots on the gray stage cloth. "I thought I had it right. I'm always up there."

"Don't we know it? And we know why: you made sure of that," said Andy Capp, unforgiveably. "Now get off the stage and get out of the way, there's a good girl. Do your courting out of school, next time."

Juliet tried to look at Birkett. Birkett looked up at the proscenium arch. The second amber flood was dead. He thought there might be a spare bulb in the box below the switchboard. If not, he would have to get one ordered tomorrow. When he looked round again, Juliet was gone, climbing awkwardly over the apron and down into the hall. The darkness took her. Andy Capp followed.

"Get on with it, rabble."

"Good night, Penthesilia," said Sir Toby.

"Before me, she's a good wench."

"She's a beagle, true-bred, and one that adores me; what o' that?"

"I was adored once, too," said Birkett.

FOR BEING GOOD

CYNTHIA RYLANT

W HAT PHILIP REMEMBERS about his grandfather are the big blue veins on the top of his hands. Philip hasn't seen the old man for five years, since he was six, and he can't remember his grandfather's eyes or teeth or ears or nose. Just hands with blue veins.

Grandfather is coming for Christmas, flying up from Florida. He is coming by himself because his wife, Philip's grandmother died, and since then he's done everything alone, including celebrating Christmas. But this year he is coming to Philip's house.

Philip isn't sure he wants his grandfather to come, but he doesn't know why he feels this way. It worries him.

In the three weeks before Christmas, Philip's mother spends a lot of time shopping for Christmas presents for his grandfather. Sometimes she drags Philip along to the department store, and she squirts colognes up and down his arms, asking him to choose the best smell. Philip can never tell one smell from the other, so he just points to a bottle and says, "He'll like that one," and she buys it.

But Philip isn't at all sure what his grandfather likes. He

doesn't know what the man likes in colognes, or ties, or socks, or pajamas—or boys. He wonders about what the old man likes in a boy.

Philip's father works for days fixing the guest room for the grandfather. He knows the man wants hardboard under his mattress, so he takes care of that. He fixes the broken runner on the rocking chair. He gives the walls a fresh coat of white paint. And he brings some old pictures out of a box—pictures of himself and his three brothers when they were little boys and Philip's grandfather was a young man. He puts them in frames on the dresser.

It is two days before Christmas when the old man finally arrives. Philip is afraid and he wants to hide in his room. He is afraid to meet the man for whom they have been preparing so long. He wishes his grandfather wouldn't come.

But just about dinnertime, he does come. The door opens and Philip's father walks in, carrying a suitcase, and behind him stands the grandfather.

Philip keeps behind his mother as they go to the front door. He tries to smile. He tries to look like a wonderful boy.

The old man is tall. But he is tired, so it seems a gentle, embarrassed sort of tallness. He wears glasses. He has wrinkles. And underneath his hat, he is bald.

What Philip thinks, when he sees him, is that the old man seems to keep behind Philip's father as they stand inside the door. He seems to try to smile. And he seems to try to look like a wonderful grandfather.

Philip thinks maybe he is going to like him.

They all have dinner together, Philip's mother and father talking too much, telling the grandfather about the work they've done on the roof, the tomatoes they'd canned in the summer, the squirrel that always robbed the bird feeder. Philip stays quiet, watching the old man. And the grandfather smiles and nods and with his fork moves his food around on his plate. He seems not to really be with them. He reminds Philip of himself when his parents make him go to church on mornings he'd rather sleep.

After dinner, the old man goes to bed. Philip helps his mother bake sugar cookies and he wonders if his grandfather would have liked to eat some of the dough. He wraps a little ball of it in foil and puts it in the refrigerator, just in case.

The next day is Christmas Eve and Philip's parents are crazily running errands, as usual. Philip's mother always remembers one more person who might like some cookies or one more neighbor who might need visiting. And Philip's father always remembers one more gallon of milk, one more bag of birdseed, one more present for his wife.

Philip spends half the day running with his mother, and the other half running with his father, so he hardly sees his grandfather at all. Somehow he senses the old man probably wants it this way.

In the evening they all go to church. Philip loves church on Christmas Eve, the dark wood and the candle glow and the Christmas story. And it is exciting to have his grandfather there. The old man looks livelier, and as they head for a pew, he catches Philip's eye and winks. Philip thinks about that wink through the whole service.

But when they return home, and as they sit in the kitchen together eating apples and drinking hot chocolate, Philip can see his grandfather's liveliness disappearing. He watches the old man slowly deflate like a leaking bicycle tire, and he doesn't know why it is happening, and he wants to stop it. He wants to pump the old man up again, to see him wink, maybe laugh.

But Philip's grandfather sags more and more until finally he goes to bed.

Philip helps his parents clean up the kitchen.

"He misses her," his father says.

"I know," answers his mother.

"Who?" Philip asks.

And they both answer: "His wife."

Philip's father looks sad then, too, and for the first time Philip remembers that his father is talking about his own parents, his own mother, who is dead.

"Well," Philip smiles, trying to cheer him up, "he's got us."

His father hugs him then and drapes the tea towel over his head.

When it is time for Philip to go to bed, leaving his parents to "listen for reindeer," he realizes he hasn't been thinking about presents that much at all. In fact, ever since his grandfather arrived, he's thought mostly about him.

Halfway up the stairs Philip turns around and goes back into the kitchen. He opens the refrigerator and takes out the foil-wrapped ball of dough.

Upstairs, he stands at his grandfather's door and listens. He hears the rocking chair squeak. He hears the old man cough. So he knocks.

The door opens. His grandfather stands in his pajamas, his bald head shining, his feet bare, his blue-veined hands clutching a framed picture.

Philip holds out the foil.

"I saved you some dough, Grandpa."

The old man unwraps the foil, looks at the ball of dough,

then pops it into his mouth.

"Pretty good dough," he says, and he smiles.

Philip gives a little laugh. He wants to say something, to talk, but he can't think of any words.

To his surprise, his grandfather motions him into the room. He offers Philip the rocking chair, then he sits on the edge of the bed. He leans over and puts the picture into Philip's hands.

"That's your father," he says.

Philip looks at the photograph. It is a dark-haired boy, like himself. He nods his head.

"When he was a boy," the old man continues, "every Christmas Eve he'd come climbing into bed with us, Florrie and me. We never told any of his brothers, 'cause you know how boys are."

Philip grins.

"He was embarrassed about it, being so scared and nervous at Christmas that he had to crawl into our bed. We laughed about it, but we never laughed in front of him."

The old man is grinning, too. But then the grin begins to weaken.

"Truth is, we liked it." He shakes his head. "We missed having a baby in the bed between us, so we liked that little boy snoring in our ears every Christmas Eve. It was a special present just for us, we told ourselves, just for being good. Good to our boys."

Philip watches the old man's eyes fall, his mouth go slack, and even the bald head seems to lose its shine. He looks at the man's big blue veins and doesn't know what to say. So he just says, "Good night and Merry Christmas."

In bed, Philip can't sleep. Though he thinks some about the presents he might get, mostly he thinks about the old man holding the picture of his little boy. A boy who crawled into bed and snored into his father's ear on Christmas Eve. A boy who was himself a gift to his parents, who had been good.

Philip lies awake and thinks about all this a long time. Then he leaves his bed and, going past his parents' room, he stands at his grandfather's door and knocks softly.

"Grandpa?" he whispers.

Inside, the old man mumbles.

Philip opens the door and stands beside the old man's bed.

"Grandpa," he whispers, "can I sleep with you?"

The old man mumbles again, then rolls himself to one side.

Philip climbs in.

"Good night, Grandpa," he says.

"Good night, son," is the answer.

THE WATER WOMAN
AND HER LOVER

RALPH PRINCE

A Guyanese legend

I T'S AN OLD ESSEQUIBO TALE they used to tell in whispers. But even as they whispered the tale they were afraid the wind might blow their whisperings into the river where the water woman lived. They were afraid the water woman might hear their whisperings and return to haunt them as she had haunted her lover.

It's a strange story. Here it is from the beginning:

There was an old koker near Parika, through which water passed to and from the Essequibo river, for drainage of the lands in the area. On moonlight nights a naked woman was often seen sitting near the koker, with her back to the road and her face to the river.

She was a fair-skinned woman, and she had long, black, shiny hair rolling over her shoulders and down her back. Below her waist she was like a fish. When the moon was bright, especially at full-moon time, you could see her sitting on the koker, combing her long, black, shiny hair. You could see very dimly just a part of her face—a side view. But if you stepped nearer to get a closer look she would disappear. Without even turning her head to see who was coming, she would plunge into the river with a splash and vanish. They called her Water Mama.

People used to come from Salem, Tuschen, Naamryck and other parts of the east bank of the Essequibo river to see this mysterious creature. They would wait in the bush near the koker from early morning, and watch to see her rise from the river. But no matter how closely they watched, they would never see her when she came from the water. For a long time they would wait, and watch the koker bathed in moonlight. Then suddenly, as if she had sprung from nowhere, the water woman would appear sitting near the koker, completely naked, facing the river, and combing her long, black hair.

There was a strong belief among the villagers in the area that riches would come to anyone who found Water Mama's comb, or a lock of her hair. So they used to stay awake all night at the koker, and then early in the morning, even before the sun rose, they would search around where she had sat combing her hair. But they never found anything. Only the water that had drained off her body remained behind—and also a strong fishy smell.

The old people said that after looking at Water Mama or searching near the koker for her hair and her comb, you were always left feeling haunted and afraid. They told stories of people found sleeping, as if in a trance, while walking away from the koker. They warned that if a man watched her too long, and searched for her hair and her comb too often, he would dream about her. And if the man loved her and she loved him, she would haunt him in his dreams. And that would be the end of him, they said, because she was a creature of the devil. These warnings did not frighten the younger and more adventurous men from the villages around. They kept coming from near and far to gaze at Water Mama. After watching her and searching for her hair and her comb, they always had that haunted, fearful feeling. And many mornings, even as they walked away from the koker, they slept, as in a trance. But still they returned night after night to stare in wonder at that strange, mysterious woman.

At last something happened—something the old people had always said would happen—a man fell in love with the water woman. Some say he was from Salem. Some say he came from Naamryck. Others say he hailed from Parika, not far from the koker. Where he came from is not definitely known; but it is certain that he was a young man, tall and dark and big, with broad shoulders. His name was John, and they called him Big John because of his size.

When Big John had first heard of Water Mama he laughed and said she was a jumbie. But as time went by he heard so many strange things about her that he became curious. And so one moonlit night he went to the koker to look at the water woman.

He had waited for nearly an hour, and watched the moonlight shining on the koker and the river. His old doubts had returned and he was about to leave when he saw something strange, something that "mek he head rise," as the old folks say when telling the story. He saw a naked woman, sitting near the koker. A moment before, he had seen no one there. Then suddenly he saw this strange woman sitting in the moonlight and combing her long, black hair. It shone brightly in the moonlight.

Big John made a few steps toward her to see her more clearly. Then suddenly she was gone. Without even turning her head around to look at him, she plunged into the river with a big splash and vanished. Where he had seen her sitting, there was a pool of water. And then arose a strong, fishy smell. A feeling of dread overcame him.

He then set out to get away from there. He tried to run but could only walk. And even as he began walking, his steps were slow and his eyes were heavy with sleep. And that is the way he went home, walking and staggering, barely able to open his eyes now and then to see where he was going, walking and sleeping, as in a trance.

The next morning when Big John awoke and remembered what he had seen and experienced the night before, he became afraid. He vowed never to go back to the koker to look at the water woman. But that night the moon rose, flooding the land in silver, glistening in the trees, sparkling on the river. He became enchanted. His thoughts turned to the riverside and the strange woman combing her long, black hair.

And so later that night he stood near the koker waiting and watching for the strange woman to appear. Just like the night before, she appeared suddenly near the koker, combing her hair in the moonlight. Big John stepped toward her but she plunged into the river and disappeared. And once again he had that feeling of dread, followed by drowsiness as he walked home.

This went on for several nights, with Big John becoming more and more fascinated as he watched the water woman combing her hair in the moonlight. After the third night he no longer felt afraid, and he walked in the pool of water she left behind. Sometimes he waited until morning and searched around for locks of her hair and her comb, but he never found them.

After a few months of this waiting and watching, Big John felt sad and lost. He had fallen in love with the strange woman. But he could not get near to her. And so he stopped going to the riverside to watch her.

When the moon had gone and the dark nights came back he began to drop her from his mind. But in another month the moon returned, flooding the land in silver, gleaming in the trees, sparkling on the river, and he remembered the water woman, and he longed to see her combing her hair again.

And on that very night the moon returned, he had a strange dream. He saw the water woman sitting near the koker, combing her long, black hair shining in the moonlight. She sat with her back to the river and her face full toward him. As she combed her hair she smiled with him, enchanting him with her beauty. He stepped forward to get a closer look, but she did not move. And so at last he saw her clearly, her bright eyes, her lovely face, her teeth sparkling as she smiled, and her body below her waist tapered off like a fish. She was the most beautiful creature he had ever seen.

He stretched out his hands to touch, and she gave him her comb and said, "Take this to remember me by."

Then she jumped into the river and disappeared.

When he awoke the next morning he remembered the dream.

He felt happy as he told his friends what he had seen in the dream. But they were afraid for him, and they warned him:

"Is haunt she hauntin' you."

"She goin' mek you dream an' dream till you don' know

wha' to do wid youself."

"When she ready she goin' do wha' she like wid you."

"Big John you better watch youself wid de water woman."

"De water woman goin' haunt you to de en'."

These warnings made Big John laugh, and he told them:

"She can' do me anyt'ing in a dream."

But they warned him again:

"You forget 'bout de water woman, but she don' forget 'bout you."

"Is you start it when you watch she so much at de koker."

"Now you 'rouse she an' she want you. Da is de story now, she want you."

Big John laughed off these warnings and told them that nothing was going to happen to him as nothing could come from a dream.

But later that day he saw something strange. It made him shiver with dread. On the floor near his bed was a comb. He could not believe his eyes. It looked very much like the comb the water woman had given to him in the dream. He wondered how a comb he had seen in a dream could get into his room.

When he told his friends about finding the comb they said:

"Is bes' for you to go 'way from here."

"Is you start it when you watch she so much at de koker."

That night he had another dream. In this dream he saw the water woman sitting in the moonlight. He stepped even closer to her than before, and she smiled with him.

For the first time since he had seen her, she was not combing her hair, and she had no comb in her hand. She pulled out a few strands of her hair and gave them to him and said, "Keep these to remember me by." And he took them in his hands and smiled with her. In another instant she was gone with a splash into the river.

The next morning Big John awoke with a smile as he remembered the dream. But as he sat up in the bed he found himself with a few strands of hair in his hands. His eyes opened wide in surprise. It was only then that he realized that he was getting caught in something strange.

And so the dreams went on, night after night. They became like magnets drawing Big John to bed early every night, and holding him fast in sleep till morning. They no longer made him feel afraid on awakening.

In one dream the water woman gave him a conch shell. On awakening the next morning he found sand on his bed and grains of sand in both hands. One night he dreamed that he and the water woman played along the river bank, splashing each other with water. The next morning he found his bed wet, and water splashed all over the room.

Big John told his friends about these dreams, and they warned him that the water woman had him under a spell. They were right, he kept on dreaming about her night after night.

Then came his last dream. The water woman stood by the riverside holding a large bundle to her bosom. She smiled and said: "You have my comb and strands of my hair. I have given you other little gifts to remember me by.

Tonight I shall give you money to make you rich. If you keep it a secret you will stay on earth and enjoy it. If you do not keep it a secret, you must come with me and be my lover forever."

She hurled the bundle to him, and then jumped into the river and was gone.

When Big John awoke the next morning he found the floor of the room covered with tens of thousands of five-dollar bills, piled up high in heaps. It took him a long time to gather them and count them. It was a vast fortune.

Big John was too excited to keep the news about the dream and the fortune it had brought all to himself. He went around the village and told some of his closest friends about it. When they went with him to his house and saw those great piles of money, their eyes bulged and their mouths opened wide in amazement.

Then they made a wild scramble for it. They fought among themselves all that afternoon for the money. Some of them got away with little fortunes. Some ran away with their pockets bulging with notes. Others were left with notes that got torn up in the scrambling and fighting. Big John himself was beaten by the others and got nothing. They ran away and left him.

What happened to Big John after that no one knows. Some say he dreamed again of the water woman that night and she took him away in the dream. Some say he went to the koker several nights to look for her but never found her, and so he drowned himself in the river. Others say that the water woman sent her water people for him, and that they took him to live with her in her home at the bottom of the river.

But if you go down to the koker near Parika on any night of the full moon, you will see the water woman sitting with her back to the road and her face to the river, combing her long, black, shiny hair in the moonlight. You will also see a tall, big man with broad shoulders standing close beside her.

THE FAVORITE

JACQUELINE WILSON

W E KNEW WHERE WE WERE with Miss Fennimore, our old art teacher. She looked the part. Her wild gray hair was always escaping her bun and coiling down her neck in question marks. As she chatted about shading and perspective she was always trying to catch up the straggly bits with tortoiseshell combs. She went in for chunky jewelry—strings of amber, clanking bangles, agate rings. She was chunky too, but she didn't seem to remember this when she bought her clothes. Her T-shirts were always too tight and her tie-dyed trousers were taut over her spreading hips. She wore sandals too. She trod from girl to girl in those awful open-toed sandals, and whenever she spoke to me I'd look down at her ridged nails and see the little corn where the sandals rubbed and feel depressed.

Mandy and Trish and the others sent her up a bit but Miss Fennimore was so good-natured she just laughed when they teased her. I didn't join in. I'm not one of the noisy naughty ones. I don't generally get noticed much even though I tag around with Mandy and Trish. I'm middling at most things and mousy to look at. Some of the teachers have difficulty remembering my name even though I've been in their classes for years.

But it was different with Miss Fennimore. It's the one thing I'm good at. Art. I don't really like the sort of art we do at school. I like my own private art, when I shut myself in my bedroom for hours on end with huge sheets of cartridge paper and my big Christmas tin of Caran D'Ache pencils and I draw imaginary lands. I people them with all sorts of weird fantastic creatures. I pretend I'm one of them, and I'm not a bit middling or mousy. But even though school art is boring I can do it OK. Mandy and Trish generally tease me far more than they do the teachers, but they both go on and on about my so-called artistic ability. Miss Fennimore was very encouraging too. She'd always spend twice the time at my desk. She said I had a real talent and she was sure I'd get into art school when I was older. She lent me some art books and gave me a whole set of National Gallery postcards.

I was grateful but embarrassed too. I'd wanted to be singled out at school and yet it made me go hot and uncomfortable. I wanted Miss Fennimore to keep on making a fuss of me and yet my tummy went tight when she approached, and I blushed when she crowded up close to me to point something out.

"Did you see Megan blush?" Mandy hissed.

"She went scarlet. She hasn't half got a crush on old Fat-Bum Fennimore," Trish tittered.

I didn't have a crush on Miss Fennimore. I didn't even like her very much, though she was so kind to me. So I had mixed feelings when she announced she was leaving at the end of the summer term. She invited me round to her flat that summer so I could see some of *her* artwork, but I made some excuse about having to help out in my mum's shop. I didn't help out much. I didn't see Mandy and Trish that much either. They went on holiday together and met these two boys and went around with them all the time. I spent most of the summer shut in my bedroom, drawing until my felt-tip pens went dry.

When school eventually started again I was curious to see who our new art teacher was. When we filed into the big hall for Assembly I looked at all the school staff standing on the stage, ready to spot the new faces. And then I saw him. We all saw him. We all stood, transfixed. We couldn't belive it, even after Miss Parish, the head, introduced him. Mr. White, our new art teacher.

We've had quite a few male teachers before, even though ours is a girls' school. But they've always been exactly the sort of men you'd imagine: beards and Hush Puppy shoes or balding and twitchy with sweat-stains on their shirts. Mr. White was young and blond and smiling. Smiling at all of us. Smiling at me. He was glancing along the rows of girls, and then he saw me and he smiled, specially for me.

That was the way it seemed, anyway. Though Mandy and Trish and the others seemed to think they'd been singled out too. Everyone was whispering all through Assembly and afterward the whole school was buzzing. It was Mr. White this, Mr. White that. How old is he? Do you think he highlights his hair? His eyes! That smile!

Hundreds of girls, all saying the same things. Hundreds of girls, all desperate for their first art lesson of the term.

"If only I was good at art!" said Mandy.

"I know," said Trish. "I can't draw for toffee either."

They both glared at me.

"You lucky swine," said Mandy.

"You'll be teacher's pet again, Megan. It's not *fair*. Oh wow! What wouldn't I give to be Mr. White's little pet," said Trish.

"Don't be daft," I said, but my heart was thudding inside my crisp school shirt.

We had a double art lesson that afternoon. The art room had already been transformed. Miss Fennimore's prim reproductions of Old Masters had all been pulled down. There were huge poster reproductions of Matisse, Picasso, Cezanne, Van Gogh, so that the walls crackled with color. There were postcards too, tacked into themed displays— portraits, pop art, landscapes. Mandy and Trish paused, eyes popping, at the nude postcards—plump pink Renoir ladies, marble Michelangelo men, anxious angular Munch girls, Hockney boys bare but for their socks.

"Is this what we're going to be painting?" Mandy spluttered.

"Who's going to do the posing then?" said Trish. "Oh boy, let's hope it's Mr. White!"

They started giggling hysterically and Mr. White shook his head at them.

"Hey, girls, cut the cackle, eh?" he said. "I thought we'd all do a self-portrait today, right? I've got some little mirrors here. Help yourselves, prop your mirror up on your desk so you can remind yourself what you look like, and then get started. A quick pencil sketch and then start splodging on some paint. I want to see what you can do."

There was a little routine groaning and a few more giggles but everyone soon settled. Mr. White was very much in control, even though he was casual and relaxed. Poor Miss Fennimore used to spend fifteen minutes or more getting everybody sorted out and started, but in next to no time everyone was peering into their mirrors and painting. Everyone but me.

I so badly wanted to show Mr. White that I could paint, that I was the one who was good at art, that I was special. But I didn't look special. I screwed up my face and my mirror image grimaced back at me. Pale, panicky, pathetic. I tried to make a bold sketch but my hand shook and had no skill. I started rubbing out my crude beginnings.

"Hey, no erasers," said Mr. White.

"But—"

He shook his head. "I want to see the way you do it first time round."

So I was stuck. I had to carry on, even though it had all gone wrong. It was terrifying knowing there was no going back. I drew such light timid lines they were scarcely visible on the paper, and when I started painting my pale water colors blurred and bled into each other.

Mr. White started wandering around the room. His wasn't the measured sandaled tread of Miss Fennimore. He bounded erratically in his sneakers, darting here and there. He laughed at Mandy's overoptimistic representation of herself as a cartoon Monroe, blonde curls and pouting lips and big bosom. He chatted to Trish for ages, showing her how to shade, leaning over her to pencil on her paper. Her portrait gained depth and Trish herself was painted pink.

I kept waiting for it to be my turn, though I dreaded what he'd say. But each time I thought he was approaching me he changed direction with a little squeak of his sneakers and started talking to some other girl. The bell had gone and we were packing up when he eventually glanced in my direction. He looked at my wishy-washy portrait and then sighed.

"I thought I said no rubbing out?"

"I didn't."

He raised his eyebrows, as if he didn't believe me. I

208

looked at my portrait too. It did look as if I'd rubbed it all over until I was hardly there.

"She really didn't, Mr. White," said Mandy.

"She's ever so good at art, Megan, isn't she?" said Trish. "She's much better than any of us. She always used to be Miss Fennimore's favorite."

"Well, I don't have favorites," said Mr. White. "Megan is a competent artist but she's got to learn to paint with conviction."

I felt as if he'd stamped all over me in his jaunty sneakers. Mandy and Trish were consoling, but I could see by the brightness of their eyes that they were also secretly thrilled. Maybe they stood more chance with Mr. White now. Because no matter what he said, all teachers had their favorites.

I decided I didn't care. Mr. White was bigheaded and arrogant and he didn't know half as much about real art as Miss Fennimore. Why should I want to be his favorite?

I tried hard to impress him every art lesson all the same. I threw away my rubber. I started to draw with a darker pencil. I mixed bright bold colors and spread them thickly on my paper. I breathed in hard and bit my lip as I worked; I so badly wanted to paint with conviction. But Mr. White generally found fault. He saw through all the little tricksy things that had thrilled Miss Fennimore. He was dismissive of my light reflections and dark shadows.

"Don't fuss so with all the flibberty bits," he said. "Paint what's there first. Go for the center. Be bold, Megan."

I was Megan the middling, Megan the mouse. I didn't know how to be bold. Though at home, shut in my bedroom, I drew a new imaginary land, a glittering golden place where I was a giant princess, and I had a prince too, a gold prince just for me, a prince made bashful by my boldness, a prince who would stride seven leagues in his sneakers just to be by my side.

I wasn't alone in my fantasies. I think every girl in my class had fallen in love with Mr. White. Stories about him circulated the cloakrooms every single day. Mr. White had put his arm round one girl. Mr. White had told another she was cute. Mr. White's first name was Tim.

Tim. I whispered it in bed at night. And then I went to sleep and dreamed about him, and my dreams were as bold as brass. But in the art room I pretended not to care. I forced myself not to look up when he came near. I carried on painting, even though my hand shook. And it was no use anyway. I simply couldn't seem to please him. He praised nearly all the other girls but he kept on pick pick picking at me.

Each art lesson seemed over in a flash, and then there was another long weary week to get through. I still saw him round and about school but they were only glimpses. Some of the girls tried following him home. He'd been spotted in shops, in pubs, in clubs. Then Mandy came rushing into school one Monday to say she'd seen him in Sainsburys on Saturday with his family.

"Yeah, honest! It *was* him. He spoke to me, for God's sake. He said, 'Hello, Mandy.' Anyway. He's got this little toddler with cute blond hair—just like his daddy. He said hello too. But his wife didn't."

"Come on, come *on*, Mandy, what's she like?"

"She looks a bit boring, actually. Youngish and her hair was a bit of a mess. She was fat too. Yeah, OK OK, I know I'*m* fat, but she's sort of lumbering. Well, she might be pregnant, I suppose. But she still doesn't look anything special. Not special enough for *him*."

I hated the idea of this wife, this child, maybe children— but they didn't stop my secret fantasies. Mr. White was still special for me. Just occasionally he'd seem to catch my eye and smile as if he knew, as if I was special too, but then the next lesson in art he'd snub me and scoff at my paintings and I'd sink back into despair.

I didn't know what sort of mark he'd give me at the end of term. Miss Fennimore had always marked me so highly. I'd got over ninety per cent in my art exam last year, and my form teacher had added a little "Well done!" at the bottom of my art report. The reports were already circulating round the teachers. After our English teacher had written hers she stopped me at the end of the lesson and asked me to take them over to the art room for Mr. White.

Mandy and Trish had rushed on ahead for their lunch. I went over to the art room on my own. Mr. White was on his own too, pinning up some surrealist pictures.

"Ah. Hi, Megan," he said, and he smiled.

I swallowed.

"Here are our reports for you to fill in, Mr. White," I said.

I handed them over hurriedly, my damp hands making faint stains on the folder.

"Don't look so worried," said Mr. White. He reached out and patted me on the shoulder. The warmth of his hand through my school blouse seared my skin. "I'm going to give you a very good report. I know I've been hard on you —but it's only because you've got such talent."

I felt as if I would faint with pleasure at his words. I turned hastily so that he couldn't see and pretended to look at the new pictures.

There was one strange dark painting of four girls in a midnight street—one lying naked on blue satin sheets, and three fully clothed in black dresses, their hair tied back with big ribbons.

"Like yours," said Mr. White softly, pulling my ponytail. "And they all look so pale, so tense. Like you, Megan."

He was so close his breath tickled my neck. I didn't know what to do, what to say. The art room seemed to slant and then spin, the colors changing like a kaleidoscope. I don't know whether I swayed or stumbled, but Mr. White was suddenly holding me. His face blurred as it came even nearer. I felt as if I were blurring too. This was my dream. But it wasn't a dream. It was real.

He did like me. I was special. I was his favorite. But this was different. It was what I wanted. But I didn't want *him* to want it. I didn't want him to want me because that stopped him being special. It made him shabby and speculative. He was my schoolteacher, a married man with a family. I was a schoolgirl.

So I forced myself to act like one, though I've never felt more grown up in my life.

"Of course I'm a bit tense, Mr. White, because I'm really worried about my report," I gabbled. "I've got to prove to my mum that I've got a chance to go to art school. She just wants me to work in the shop with her, you see . . ."

I chatted on desperately, and maybe he did start to see. He blinked and took a step backward and started talking too. Relaxed and casual as ever, but I'd seen a flicker of fear in his eyes. He was scared he'd misjudged things, scared I might tell.

But I didn't breathe a word. Nothing had really happened after all—although I knew I could turn it into an elaborate story for Mandy and Trish. It would make them take me seriously at last. But I didn't want to talk about it. I was already wishing it had never happened. Wishing there was some way of rubbing it all out.

TELLING STORIES

MAEVE BINCHY

PEOPLE ALWAYS SAID that Irene had total recall. She seemed to remember the smallest details of things they had long forgotten—the words of old pop songs, the shades of old lipsticks, minute-by-minute reconstructions of important events like Graduation Day, or people's weddings. If ever you wanted a step-by-step account of times past, they said to each other: ask Irene.

Irene rarely took herself through the evening before the day she was due to be married. But if she had to then she could have done it with no difficulty. It wasn't hard to remember the smells: the lilac in the garden, the polish on all the furniture, the orange blossom in the house. She even remembered the rich smell of the hand cream that she was massaging carefully into her hands when she heard the doorbell ring. It must be a late present, she thought, or possibly yet another fussy aunt who had come up from the country for the ceremony and arrived like a homing pigeon at the house.

She was surprised to hear Andrew's voice, talking to her younger sister downstairs. Andrew was meant to be at his home dealing with all his relations just as Irene had been doing. He had an uncle, a priest, flying in from the African Missions to assist at the wedding. Andrew's grandmother was a demanding old lady who regarded every gathering as in some way centering around her; Irene was surprised that Andrew had been allowed to escape.

Rosemary, her sister and one of the bridesmaids, had no interest in anything apart from the possible appearance of a huge spot on her face. She waved Andrew airily up the stairs.

"She's been up there titivating herself for hours," Irene heard her say. Before she had time to react to Rosemary's tactlessness, Irene heard Andrew say "Oh God," in a funny, choked sort of voice, and before he even came into the room, she knew something was very wrong.

Andrew's face was as white as the dress that hung between sheets of tissue paper on the outside of the big mahogany wardrobe. His hands shook and trembled like the branches of the beautiful laburnum tree outside her window, the yellow blossom shaking in the summer breeze.

He tried to take her hand but she was covered in hand cream. Irene decided that somehow it was imperative that she keep rubbing the cream still further in. It was like not walking on the crack in the road: if she kept massaging her hands then he couldn't take them in his, and he couldn't tell her what awful thing he was about to tell her.

On and on she went rhythmically, almost hypnotically, as if she were pulling on tight gloves. Her hands never stopped moving; her face never moved at all.

He fumbled for words, but Irene didn't help him.

The words came eventually, tumbling over each other, contradicting each other even, punctuated with apology and self-disgust. It wasn't that there was anyone else, Lord no, and it wasn't even as if he had stopped loving her, in many ways he had never loved her more than now, looking at her and knowing that he was destroying all their dreams and their hopes, but he had thought about it very seriously, and the truth was that he wasn't ready, he wasn't old enough, maybe technically he was old enough, but in his heart he didn't feel old enough to settle down, he wasn't certain enough that this was the Right Thing. For either of them, he added hastily, wanting Irene to know that it was in her interests as well as his.

On and on, she worked the cream into her hands and wrists; even a little way up her arms.

She sat impassively on her little blue bedroom stool, her frilly dressing table behind her. There were no tears, no tantrums. There were not even any words. Eventually he could speak no more.

"Oh Irene, say something for God's sake, tell me how much you hate me, what I've done to your life." He almost begged to be railed against.

She spoke slowly, her voice was very calm. "But of course I don't hate you," she said, as if explaining something to a slow-witted child. "I love you, I always will, and let's look at what you've done to my life . . . You've changed it certainly . . ." Her eyes fell on the wedding dress.

Andrew started again. Guilt and shame poured from him in a torrent released by her unexpected gentleness. He would take it upon himself to explain to everyone, he would tell her parents now. He would explain everything to the guests, he would see that the presents were returned. He would try to compensate her family financially for all the expense they had gone to. If everyone thought this was the right thing to do he would go abroad, to a faraway place like Australia or Canada or Africa . . . somewhere they needed young lawyers, a place where nobody from here need ever look at him again and remember all the trouble he had caused.

And then suddenly he realized that he and he alone was doing the talking; Irene sat still, apart from those curious hand movements, as if she had not heard or understood what he was saying. A look of horror came over his face: perhaps she did not understand.

"I mean it, Irene," he said simply. "I really do mean it, you know, I wish I didn't."

"I know you mean it." Her voice was steady, her eyes were clear. She did understand.

Andrew clutched at a straw. "Perhaps *you* feel the same. Perhaps we *both* want to get out of it? Is that what you are saying?" He was so eager to believe it, his face almost shone with enthusiasm.

But there was no quarter here. In a voice that didn't shake, with no hint of a tear in her eye, Irene said that she loved him and would always love him. But that it was far better, if he felt he couldn't go through with it, that this should be discovered the night before the marriage, rather than the night after. This way at least one of them would be free to make a different marriage when the time came.

"Well both of us, surely?" Andrew was bewildered.

Irene shook her head. "I can't see myself marrying anyone else but you," she said. There was no blame, regret, accusation. Just a statement.

In the big house, where three hundred guests were expected tomorrow, it was curiously silent. Perhaps the breeze had died down; they couldn't even hear the flapping of the edges of the marquee on the lawn.

The silence was too long between them. But Andrew knew she was not going to break it. "So what will we do? First, I mean?" he asked her.

She looked at him pleasantly as if he had asked what record he should put on the player. She said nothing.

"Tell our parents, I suppose, yours first. Are they downstairs?" he suggested.

"No, they're over at the golf club, they're having a little reception or drink or something for those who aren't coming tomorrow."

"Oh God," Andrew said.

There was another silence.

"Do you think we should go and tell *my* parents then? Grandmother will need some time to get adjusted . . ."

Irene considered this. "Possibly," she said. But it was unsatisfactory.

"Or maybe the caterers," Andrew said. "I saw them bustling around setting things up . . ." His voice broke. He seemed about to cry. "Oh God, Irene, it's a terrible mess."

"I know," she agreed, as if they were talking about a rain cloud or some other unavoidable irritation to the day.

"And I suppose I should tell Martin, he's been fussing so much about the etiquette of it all and getting things in the right order. In a way he may be relieved . . ." Andrew gave a nervous little laugh but hastily corrected himself. "But sorry, of course, mainly sorry, of course, very, very sorry that things haven't worked out."

"Yes. Of course," Irene agreed politely.

"And the bridesmaids? Don't you think we should tell Rosemary now, and Catherine? And that you should ring Rita and tell her . . . and tell her . . . that . . . well that . . ."

"Tell her what, exactly?"

"Well, tell her that we've changed our minds . . ."

"That you've changed your mind, to be strictly honest," Irene said.

"Yes, but you agree," he pleaded.

"What do I agree?"

"That if it is the Wrong Thing to do, then it were better we know now than tomorrow when it's all too late and we are man and wife till death . . ." his voice ran out.

"Ah yes, but don't you see, I don't think we *are* doing the Wrong Thing getting married."

"But you agreed . . ." He was in a panic.

"Oh, of course I agreed, Andrew, I mean what on earth would be the point of not agreeing? Naturally we can't go through with it. But that's not to say that *I'm* calling it off."

"No, no, but does that matter as much as telling people . . . I mean now that we know that it won't take place, isn't it unfair to people to let them think that it will?"

218

"Yes and no."

"But we can't have them making the food, getting dressed . . ."

"I know." She was thoughtful.

"I want to do what's best, what's the most fair," Andrew said. And he did, Irene could see that, in the situation which he had brought about, he still wanted to be fair.

"Let's see," she suggested. "Who is going to be most hurt by all this?"

He thought about it. "Your parents probably, they've gone to all this trouble . . ." He waved toward the garden where three hundred merrymakers had planned to stroll.

"No, I don't think they're the most hurt."

"Well, maybe my uncle, the whole way back from Africa and he had to ask permission from a bishop. Or my grandmother . . . or the bridesmaids. They won't get a chance to dress up." Andrew struggled to be fair.

"I think that I am the one who will be most hurt." Irene's voice wasn't even slightly raised. It was as if she had given the problem equally dispassionate judgment.

"I mean, my parents have other daughters. There'll be Rosemary and Catherine, one day they'll have weddings. And your uncle, the priest . . . well he'll have a bit of a holiday. No, I think I am the one who is most upset, I'm not going to marry the man I love, have the life I thought I was going to.

"I know, I know." He sounded like someone sympathizing over a bereavement.

"So I thought that perhaps you'd let me handle it *my* way."

"Of course, Irene, that's why I'm here, whatever you say."

"I say we shouldn't tell anyone anything. Not tonight."

"I won't change my mind, in case that's what you're thinking."

"Lord no, why should you? It's much too serious to be flitting about, chopping and changing."

219

He handed their future into her hands. "Do it whatever way you want. Just let me know and I'll do it." He was prepared to pay any price to get the wedding called off.

But Irene didn't allow herself the time to think about that. "Let me be the one not to turn up," she said. "Let me be seen to be the partner who had second thoughts. That way at least I get out of it with some dignity."

He agreed. Grooms had been left standing at the altar before. He would always say afterward that he had been greatly hurt but he respected Irene's decision.

"And you won't tell *anyone*?" she made him promise.

"Maybe Martin?" he suggested.

"Particularly not Martin, he'd give the game away. In the church you must be seen to be waiting for me."

"But your father and mother . . . is it fair to leave it to the last minute?"

"They'd prefer to think that I let you down rather than the other way. Who wants a daughter who has been abandoned by the groom?"

"It's not that . . ." he began.

"I *know* that, silly, but not everyone else does." She had stopped creaming her hands. They talked like old friends and conspirators. The thing would only succeed if nobody had an inkling.

"And afterward . . ." He seemed very eager to know every step of her plan.

"Afterward . . ." Irene was thoughtful. "Oh, afterward we can go along being friends . . . until you meet someone else. . . People will admire you, think you are very forgiving, too tolerant even . . . There'll be no awkwardness. No embarrassment."

Andrew stood at the gate of the big house to wave good-bye; she sat by her window under the great laburnum tree and waved back. She was a girl in a million. What a pity he hadn't met her later. Or proposed to her later, when he was ready to be married. His stomach lurched at the thought of the mayhem they were about to unleash the following day. He went home with a heavy heart to hear stories of the Missions from his uncle the priest, and tales of long-gone grandeur from his grandmother.

Martin had read many books on being best man. Possibly too many.

"It's only natural for you to be nervous," he said to Andrew at least forty times. "It's only natural for you to worry about your speech, but remember the most important thing is to thank Irene's parents for giving her to you."

When they heard the loud sniffs from Andrew's grandmother, the best man had soothing remarks also. "It's only natural for elderly females to cry at weddings," he said.

Andrew stood there, his stomach like lead. Since marriage was instituted, no groom had stood like this in the certain knowledge that his bride was not just a little late, or held up in traffic, or adjusting her veil—all the excuses that Martin was busy hissing into his ear.

He felt a shame like he had never known, allowing all these three hundred people to assemble in a church for a ceremony that would not take place. He looked fearfully at the parish priest, and at his own uncle. It took some seconds for it to sink in that the congregation had risen to its feet, and that the organist had crashed into the familiar chords of "Here Comes The Bride."

He turned like any groom turns and saw Irene, perfectly at ease on her father's arm, smiling to the left and smiling to the right.

With his mouth wide open and his face whiter than the dress she wore, he looked into her eyes. He felt Martin's fingers in his ribs and he stepped forward to stand beside her.

Despite her famous recall, Irene never told that story to anyone. She only talked about it once to Andrew, on their honeymoon, when he tried to go over the events himself. And in all the years that followed, it had been *so* obvious that she had taken the right decision, run the right risk and realized that their marriage was the Right Thing, there was no point in talking about it at all.

Acknowledgments

The publisher would like to thank the copyright holders for permission to reproduce the following copyright material:

Vivien Alcock: John Johnson (Authors' Agent) Limited, London for *Cinderella Girl* from *In Between: Stories of Leaving Childhood* edited by Miriam Hodgson, Methuen Children's Books, 1994. Copyright © 1994 Vivien Alcock. **Daisy Ashford:** Random House U.K. Ltd., London for *A Proposale* from *The Young Visiters*, Chatto & Windus, 1919. Copyright © 1919 Daisy Ashford. **Maeve Binchy:** Christine Green (Authors' Agent), London for *Telling Stories*. Copyright © Maeve Binchy. **Betsy Byars:** Viking Penguin, a division of Penguin Books USA Inc. for *The Missing Vital Organ* from *Bingo Brown and the Language of Love*, Viking Penguin, 1989. Copyright © 1989 Betsy Byars. **Adèle Geras:** Laura Cecil Literary Agency for *The Green Behind the Glass* from *The Green Behind the Glass, Love Stories*, Hamish Hamilton Children's Books, 1982. Copyright © 1982 Adèle Geras. **Paul Jennings:** Penguin Books Australia Ltd., Melbourne for *Lucky Lips* from *Unreal!*, Penguin Books Australia Ltd., 1985. Copyright © 1985 Paul Jennings. **Diana Wynne Jones:** Laura Cecil Literary Agency for *The Girl Who Loved the Sun* from *Heartache*, edited by Miriam Hodgson, Methuen Children's Books, 1990. Copyright © 1990 Diana Wynne Jones. **Geraldine McCaughrean:** Oxford University Press for *The Plate: A Question of Values*, an extract from *A Pack of Lies*, OUP, 1988. Copyright © 1988 Geraldine McCaughrean. **Jan Mark:** David Higham Associates Ltd. for *I Was Adored Once, Too* from *Is Anyone There?*, Penguin, 1978. Copyright © 1978 Jan Mark. **Guy de Maupassant:** *A Railway Story* reprinted from *A Day in the Country and Other Stories* by Guy de Maupassant, translated by David Coward, World Classics, 1990. Copyright © 1990 David Coward. **Ann Pilling:** Viking Penguin, a division of Penguin Books USA Inc. for *The Fat Girl's Valentine* (ch. 13 from *The Big Pink*), Viking Penguin USA, 1987. Copyright © 1987 Ann Pilling and David Higham Associates Ltd. for *Billie* from *Love Them, Hate Them* edited by Tony Bradman, Methuen Children's Books 1991. Copyright © 1991 Ann Pilling. **James Reeves:** Laura Cecil Literary Agency for *Orpheus and Eurydice* from *Heroes and Monsters: Legends of Ancient Greece*, Blackie, 1969. Copyright © 1969 The Estate of James Reeves. **Barbara Robinson:** Faber and Faber Ltd., London for an extract (ch. 7) from *The Worst Kids in the World* (Hamlyn 1976) first published in Great Britain as *The Best Christmas Pageant Ever*, Faber and Faber, 1974. Copyright © 1967, 1972, Barbara Robinson. **Cynthia Rylant:** Orchard Books for *For Being Good* from *Silver Packages and Other Stories*, Orchard 1987. Copyright © 1987 Cynthia Rylant. **Kate Walker:** Kate Walker, Sydney for *Love Letters* from *State of the Heart* compiled by P. E. Mathews, Omnibus Books, Adelaide, 1988. Copyright © 1988 Kate Walker. **Jacqueline Wilson:** David Higham Associates, London for *The Favorite* from *In Between: Stories of Leaving Childhood*, edited by Miriam Hodgson, Methuen Children's Books, 1994. Copyright © 1994 Jacqueline Wilson. **Paul and Bonnie Zindel:** HarperCollins Publishers for an extract from *A Star for the Latecomer*. Copyright © 1980 Bonnie Zindel and Zindel Productions, Inc.

Every effort has been made to obtain permission to reproduce copyright material, but there may be cases where we have been unable to trace a copyright holder. The publisher will be happy to correct any errors or omissions in future printings.

Titles in the Story Library Series

ADVENTURE STORIES

Chosen by Clive King
Illustrated by Brian Walker

BALLET STORIES

Chosen by Harriet Castor
Illustrated by Sally Holmes

FANTASY STORIES

Chosen by Diana Wynne Jones
Illustrated by Robin Lawrie

FUNNY STORIES

Chosen by Michael Rosen
Illustrated by Tony Blundell

GHOST STORIES

Chosen by Robert Westall
Illustrated by Sean Eckett

GROWING UP STORIES

Chosen by Betsy Byars
Illustrated by Robert Geary

HEROIC STORIES

Chosen by Anthony Masters
Illustrated by Chris Molan

HORROR STORIES

Chosen by Susan Price
Illustrated by Harry Horse

HORSE STORIES

Chosen by Christine Pullein-Thompson
Illustrated by Victor Ambrus

LOVE STORIES

Chosen by Ann Pilling
Illustrated by Aafke Brouwer

MYTHS AND LEGENDS

Retold by Anthony Horowitz
Illustrated by Francis Mosley

SCIENCE FICTION STORIES

Chosen by Edward Blishen
Illustrated by Karin Littlewood

THUNDERING HOOVES

Chosen by Christine Pullein-Thompson
Illustrated by Victor Ambrus